I0739129

Attack ON THE CLAUSE

THE Clause
REBELLION
Elizabeth Lee Sorrell

Attack **ON THE CLAUSE**

Elizabeth Lee Sorrell

trading as

Yarbrough House Publishing, Inc.

Trading as Yabrough House Publishing, Inc.
For information please email
info@yarbroughhousepublishing.com

www.YarbroughHousePublishing.com

ISBN-978-0-9995800-1-1

First Edition.

Printed in the United States of America

Acknowledgements

I'd like to thank my family who really do all the hard work. While I sit back and make up fanciful stories, my family stays busy proofing, formatting, illustrating, crunching numbers, and taking care of all the "business stuff." All I do is play with my imagination, but my family works hard to bring life to my stories.

Chapter One

Things got crazy after Wynter left the South Pole with Mrs. Clause of all people. It was a shock to find out that Wynter was a Clause, but it didn't change who she was, the person she was inside. It didn't change the way Noah felt about her either. He still loved her.

Not everyone felt the same, though. The North Pole had been enemies of the South Pole for generations. The Clauses had always been considered the root of all evil as far as the South Pole people were concerned, but Noah didn't care, not if it included Wynter. They were friends. Wynter was a good friend, and that was what mattered.

Everyone in the South Pole was paranoid after Wynter left. Anyone who had not lived their whole lives in the South Pole were suddenly suspicious. Most people had lived their whole lives in the South Pole, but the ones who had not, like Anthony, were now under scrutiny.

Security was cracked down. People felt vulnerable after Wynter's so called invasion. Others were convinced that she had been there in the South Pole for nefarious reasons. A spy, some called her. She must have been there for some foul sabotage they would say.

Noah was shocked by all the hate. He was surrounded by hate. He knew there would be some, okay a lot, who hated Wynter simply because she was a Clause. He expected that from the people who hadn't known Wynter, but he never expected it from his own family.

Wynter had been Ethan's best friend of sorts. He was as close to her as he was anyone, and he certainly spent more time with her than he did his other friends. Their parents had spent countless hours worrying about Wynter like as if she was one of their own kids. Noah had honestly expected his family to stand up for Wynter. At the very least he had not expected them to get caught up in all the hate and prejudice. As it turned out, Ethan and his parents were just as mad about what happened as anyone, maybe more so. They felt that Wynter had tricked them and used them.

Things were no easier on Anthony. Because he and Wynter had been close, people believed that he must have been in league with her. How easily they forget that Noah and Ethan had been close to Wynter as well. Anthony was an outsider, though, and suddenly that made a difference. No one outright asked Anthony to leave, yet they all made sure he was miserable.

It wasn't long before Anthony decided to leave. He said he had to go find Wynter. Noah understood. He did, but at thirteen years old, he was jealous. He loved Wynter. Of course he loved Wynter, but at that age he still believed that he was in love with Wynter. He couldn't see then that Anthony was in love with her too and that she was in love with Anthony.

Anthony left him in charge of Roscoe. Roscoe was Wynter's pet polar bear. No one besides Anthony and Noah knew about Roscoe. The bear could understand people. That kind of magic was well beyond any of the South Pole people. No, only a Clause would be capable of something like that.

Noah loved caring for Roscoe while it lasted. Roscoe was with Wynter now in the North Pole where she lived with Anthony. They were married now, and the last time Noah had seen them Wynter was pregnant with their first child. They really were kind of perfect together. Wynter had even granted Anthony's fondest Christmas wish. He didn't like being a vampire, and Wynter somehow changed that. Clause magic, Noah didn't pretend to understand it, but it was fascinating.

Noah didn't tell Anthony and Wynter then, but things were only getting worse in the South Pole. The hate was only growing, and there were too many people who wanted revenge for what Wynter had done.

What had she done, really? She had been kind and polite. She had been a good friend. She had not caused any trouble for anyone. In fact, everyone was quick to forget that when Mrs. Clause launched a fireball at a crowd of South Polers, it was Wynter who had stopped the fireball.

Now there was only a small group of them who were able to see through all the hate and prejudice, a very small, young group. Noah had quickly become their unspoken leader, which was exactly what he had not wanted to tell Anthony and Wynter. They would worry about him leading a rebel group.

That's what they were, rebels. They didn't consider themselves rebels. They loved the South Pole. They just didn't see why the South Pole and the North Pole couldn't get along. In the eyes of everyone else that made them rebels. In his family's eyes that made him a rebel and a trouble maker. It tended to make things tense around home.

"It's nearly Christmas Eve," Ethan pointed out.

"Yeah, so?" Noah replied.

"You going to disappear again this year?"

"I might. I told you last year where I was."

"With the animals. Right."

"I'm a ranger, Ethan. It's not exactly unheard of for me to be out monitoring the wildlife. Where did you think I was?"

"I know, the youngest ranger in over sixty years."

"What do you want Ethan?"

"You know there were rumors that Anthony had been spotted around this time last year."

"So what if he had? Anthony was our friend."

"Things change."

"Yeah they do. I've got to get to work. Could you hurry up and get to your point?"

"It's just odd that Anthony shows up just before Christmas and you disappear on Christmas Eve."

"I was working, Ethan, like I need to be doing now. Is there anything else?"

"No, just know that I'm keeping an eye on you," Ethan warned.

"Just like old times, huh? That's great, Ethan. I'll see you later then."

Noah hated it that Ethan didn't trust him anymore. He hated it even more that he had to lie to his brother, but Ethan wouldn't understand about him visiting Wynter last year.

There were those who didn't think Noah should be allowed to be a ranger, didn't think he should be trusted. Ethan was one of those. It didn't matter that there was no one better with the animals than Noah. It didn't matter how many times he had protected the South Pole people from being detected by humans or how hard he'd worked to keep their secret. None of that mattered right now, because Noah was late for work.

Today's assignment wasn't a hard one. It wasn't a ferocious animal, but they sure were cute. The arctic hare might be plentiful in the north, but it had been a long time since they had been seen in the South Pole. Against all odds, a family of arctic hares were spotted

right here in the South Pole! Now it was up to Noah to see to it that they thrive, and he couldn't be happier.

Hares were similar to rabbits, but they weren't rabbits. The biggest difference was that the hares are longer. They are a bit taller with longer ears. For the most part hares ate woody plants since that was easier to find in the extreme cold terrains, but that didn't mean the hares didn't enjoy carrots. It would be like a treat for them, so that was exactly what Noah was going to use to lure them.

Noah walked out to the area where they knew the hares were hiding. He sat down on the snow and ice and placed carrots in a circle all around him. Then he waited. The hares were a bit skittish, and it took a long time, but finally they poked their noses out. Noah counted ten. They were close to one another, but they weren't together.

It reminded Noah of the way he was with his family these days. They lived close in proximity, but they weren't close emotionally any longer. They still went through many of the motions, but they just weren't the family they once were.

Noah waited patiently as the hares slowly crept out one step at a time. He spent all morning long sitting waiting on the hares, but it was worth it. Finally they crept close enough to reach the carrots.

One hare paused to watch Noah. He held perfectly still, yet the hare still raced back for his hiding spot. Two of the hares sniffed the carrots before following the first hare's example and fleeing. Another hare sniffed the first carrot she got to. She moved to the next and sniffed it as well. After sniffing the third carrot, she nibbled just a bit. She sniffed the carrot again then drug it off with her. It was a slow go for a small hare to drag the whole carrot away. Perhaps next time Noah should consider bringing carrot sticks or baby carrots. Not all of these hares were full grown yet, and it seemed the younger ones were among the braver.

Six more hares sunk their teeth deep into the carrots and drug them away while the last hare watched curiously. When all the other hares were out of sight, the last hare turned his stare on Noah. He twitched his little nose as he studied Noah. It was adorable. It was a picture perfect moment, one that Wynter could have captured with breathtaking quality.

Wynter loved taking pictures. She was good at it too. Some of Noah's favorite pictures he had hanging around his small cabin were ones that Wynter had taken when she was here. It had amazed Noah then how she captured the essence of a moment, and that was before he saw all the photos of Roscoe that were hanging around Wynter's cave.

Yes, he said cave. As it turned out, Wynter had used magic to make a warm, cozy home out of a cave. That was yet another example of Clause magic, so of course, no one else knows about the cave. Noah can't get inside anymore. The only reason he was ever able to get inside was because he had entered with Anthony, who was allowed to pass through the magical entrance.

Noah had not met Roscoe yet the first time Anthony took Noah into Wynter's cave. There were so many pictures of Roscoe everywhere. In some he looked rather tame, cute even. In others he looked ferocious, on the prowl or teeth bared swooping in for the kill. The photo that most caught Noah's attention, though, was hanging over her bed. It was a picture of himself with Ethan, and everything in the background was blurred out.

It wasn't as adventurous as the photos of wildlife, but where it hung said a lot about where Wynter's heart was. Why couldn't anyone else see her the way Noah saw her?

That picture was long gone somewhere hanging in the North Pole Noah imagined, safe and sound with Wynter.

Movement caught Noah's eye and brought him back to present day. The last hare hopped tentatively to a carrot. He, too, paused to study Noah, but then he bent his head and started gnawing on the carrot. The hare stayed right there until it finished off the carrot. Everything looked good with the hares, and Noah was satisfied. After that last hare disappeared from sight, Noah stood with a sigh and walked back to his truck.

Chapter Two

Wynter's parents were expecting her in five minutes at their house for dinner. Mom said that Dad had some big news to share. "Anthony, where is Noel?" Wynter asked.

"She's out back with Roscoe."

Wynter stared at Anthony dumbfounded. Noel, Anthony and Wynter's almost one year old daughter, was easily Roscoe's favorite person in the whole world, so Wynter wasn't at all worried about Noel playing with a huge polar bear. She was, however, worried about her daughter who was dressed for dinner with the grandparents playing outside in the backyard.

Noel was dressed in the cutest little Santa outfit. It had a red top with white fur trim and a black belt that sported a bow in front. Red booties on white leggings kept her legs nice and warm, and a Santa hat finished off the look. It was sure to make her parents smile, and now those white leggings were going to filthy.

"Anthony, she was clean," Wynter told him exasperated.

"She's adorable. Your parents won't be able to resist her in anything she wears."

"I know, but it's her first Christmas. I just want everything to be perfect."

"Then let her have fun. Let her be a child and enjoy this Christmas," Anthony suggested as he stuffed a cookie in his mouth.

"Fine, and stop eating cookies. You'll ruin your appetite."

"That will never happen," Anthony said with a big grin.

It seemed like Anthony was always eating cookies. Sometimes Wynter thought Anthony ate more cookies than her dad.

"Okay, let's just get Noel, and hurry up to Mom and Dad's."

Wynter walked out the back door and paused when she saw Roscoe and Noel. Anthony plowed into her from

behind thanks to the sudden stop. He wrapped his arms around her to keep her from pitching forward.

"What's wrong?" Anthony asked as he kissed Wynter's neck underneath her ear.

Wynter pointed towards Roscoe and Noel and stayed wrapped warmly in Anthony's arms to watch. Noel was crawling across the backyard. Roscoe was crouched behind her crawling on his belly, following Noel.

Anthony had put a tall fence around the backyard as soon as Noel started crawling with a gate big enough for Roscoe to come and go. When Noel reached the fence she turned around, and Roscoe followed suit. This put Roscoe in the lead. He continued to belly crawl back the way they had come with Noel following him.

"How long have they been doing this?" Wynter asked.

"Oh, a few minutes. They just keep going back and forth."

Wynter smiled at the game a little sorry she had to break it up. "Noel, come on. It's time to go to Gam and Papa's."

Noel squealed and crawled faster toward Wynter and Anthony. Roscoe plopped onto his side and whined.

"It's okay, big fella'. We'll be back," Anthony offered the pouting polar bear.

It was a short walk over the snow and ice to her parents' house, and Wynter's mom was there to greet them at the door. "There's my girl! Come see Gam," she cooed as she took Noel from Anthony's arms.

"Hey, sweetheart," Wynter's dad whispered as he kissed her cheek.

"Hi, Daddy."

"Anthony."

"Hey, Santa." Anthony always called Wynter's dad Santa. The wonder of meeting Santa had never worn off for Anthony. Santa had tried a few times to convince Anthony to call him dad, but Anthony insisted on Santa.

"So, Daddy, what's this big news that pulled you away from the naughty and nice list so close to Christmas?" Wynter asked.

"No, now, let's sit down to eat first," Mom said.

"I'll tell you while we eat," Santa agreed.

"You look so precious, Noel, just like your papa," Mom smiled at Noel's little Santa outfit, "but what happened to your knees? They are soaked."

"She was crawling around in the backyard with Roscoe," Wynter explained.

"Is she still crawling around?" Santa asked.

"Yeah, I guess she figures it's faster than toddling around on two feet. Sometimes I wonder if we're letting her hang out with Roscoe and the reindeer too much," Anthony admitted.

"Oh, you worry too much, Anthony. Wynter hung out with the reindeer all the time as a child, and she turned out just fine," Santa replied.

"Yeah, she did," Anthony said with a fond smile at his wife.

"All right, dinner's on the table. Let's eat," Mom told them.

Once everyone was settled and plates were served, Wynter pushed her dad, "Daddy, what's going on?"

Santa sat his fork down on his plate, took a deep breath, and let it out on a sigh. "Well... I've decided this is going to be my last year. I'm going to retire."

"Oh... We..." Anthony stuttered. "I guess I thought we'd have more time before Wynter took over. We were talking about having more kids. It's important to Wynter, to us, that Noel not be an only child."

Wynter cleared her throat and tried to discreetly shake her head at her husband.

"What... Am I missing something here?"

Santa and Wynter shared a nervous look. As a result, Anthony looked around the table with a look that portrayed both confusion and fear.

"What neither of these two have the guts to tell you is that Wynter won't be taking over the job of Santa," Mom explained.

"Then who?"

"You."

"Me?"

"The job of Santa is always passed down to a male," Wynter told him.

"Oh yeah, I remember you mentioning that once."

"Yeah."

"And," Santa added, "I was already doing the job of Santa when we had Wynter. You can still have kids. Right, sweetheart?"

"That's right," Wynter agreed.

"Me as Santa?" Anthony marveled.

"I'll train you over this next year, and we'll be here to answer any questions you might have," Santa offered in a desperate plea.

"Wow... I... I would be Santa?"

"You'll be a great Santa," Wynter encouraged. She kissed his cheek and added, "Besides, you'd get all the cookies you could eat in one night."

"Wow."

"You already said that."

"I know, but wow."

"I think that's a yes," Wynter smiled at her dad.

"It's amazing, but... what were the odds that the next Santa would be a former vampire?"

"About the same odds that Santa's daughter would fall in love with the one vampire that didn't want to be a vampire," Mom said gently. "Miracles happen every day."

"But," Anthony turned concerned eyes to Wynter, "is this what you want?"

"I do, Anthony. I think it's wonderful."

"Good," Santa said with a ring of finality. "I'm glad that's finished."

Chapter Three

"Calm down," Noah nearly shouted over all the din. "Would you all just lower your voice? Now, what's going on?"

Noah had been on the phone with his mom promising that he would be there for Christmas Eve. She wanted to start some sort of new tradition, but what she really wanted was to keep tabs on where Noah went. If that was what it took for his family to trust him just a little, then that was fine. He'd be there for Christmas, Christmas Eve, and whenever else they thought they needed to put eyes on him.

Unfortunately, the phone call had made him late for a meeting with other like-minded South Polers. They were a small group of only thirteen. Even less were willing to do anything about the way things were, but

they all believed that this rivalry between the North and the South had gone on long enough. If no one could even remember what the feud was about, what were they arguing about?

The Clause's were substantially more powerful. The South Pole magic dwarfed in comparison to the Clause's. It was possible that jealousy had started all the trouble. People can do some pretty stupid stuff when they let jealousy rule their lives, stupid things like starting a war.

The North and South Poles were the only two places on Earth where you found magic, other than demonic magic like the vampires. It wasn't too farfetched to imagine that once upon a time the two people groups were family, distant family now. There was no end of stupid stuff that could tear families apart. Somewhere along the line the two groups simply forgot that they were ever family.

Maybe the South Pole people used to work for the Clause's. Some disgruntled employee started firing up other employees until a group at last left and ended up in the South Pole. Stubborn people won't let go of past grievances, and before you know it everyone has forgotten what the original grievance was or even that there was one.

There were no end to the theories for what started the rivalry, but each theory boiled down to stupidity. Whatever the reason for the feud, it didn't change where they were now.

Now Noah was standing in the middle of an old abandoned shed surrounded by twelve other South Polers arguing.

"I'm telling you they're up to something," Eddie said frantically. Eddie was a slightly portly kid who had a video game obsession. Like everyone else who had joined their ragtag team, he thought the rivalry between the North and South Poles was outdated and unfounded. He was always paranoid about things he claimed were going down as a result of the rivalry. He was a natural conspiracy theorist, but he was far too frightened to ever make a public stand. When things came to a head, and Noah was sure they would, Eddie would be of little use.

"You always think they're up to something," Stewart combated. Stewart had very strong opinions about the uselessness of the feud, but he absolutely did not want conflict. He refused to be confrontational claiming that it would rip their families apart.

It likely will. It would certainly cause a rift in the South Pole, and it was just as likely that families would

be torn apart as well. As family members take opposing sides, families would never be the same.

"Yeah," came several voices as the chaos rose again.

"Hey, calm down. The last thing we need is to get caught in here and try to explain what's going on," Noah asserted.

"You don't have any proof," Everett pointed out. Everett was another one who didn't want to be involved in any conflict. He called himself a realist, claiming there were too few of them to ever make a difference. He said that making a ruckus would only cause unneeded strife, and besides the North Pole was too far away to ever be a real problem.

"That's true," Blossom agreed. Blossom was a pacifist. She hated confrontation, and she would never dream of getting into a heated debate about anything with anyone. Still even she could see that this feud with the North Pole was pointless.

"That doesn't matter," Eddie continued undeterred. "I know they are up to something. They're gathering steam for something big. I just don't know what."

"Then how do you know it's anything at all?" Enoch asked. In all likelihood Enoch agreed with Eddie, but

Enoch liked to play devil's advocate. He'd question anything, wanted to stay on top of things. He looked at it like a puzzle that needed to be solved. He figured if he looked at it from every angle and each viewpoint he would be prepared for anything that could be thrown at him.

"He doesn't," Owen piped in. Noah wondered sometimes if Owen agreed with the rest of the crew at all. He didn't hate the Clauses, but that was about as far as the similarities went. Owen didn't care what the others thought about the Clauses or what they did about it. All he knew is that he didn't want to be a part of it. His indifference might as well have been the same as joining the feud himself.

Declan rolled his eyes, "Of course they're planning something. They've been working toward just that since the night Mrs. Clause showed up in that overgrown sleigh." Declan's family was obsessed with bringing down the Clauses, and their obsession drove Declan to an obsession of his own. Some people called him a hot head, but that wasn't the case at all. He wasn't fast to anger, yet he wouldn't back down from a fight if one came knocking.

"The question is what we are going to do about it," Vivienne enthused. Vivienne was tall and very slender. Her build was Amazonian-like, but she was all South Pole. Vivienne was a tomboy through and through and just itching to put an end to the nonsense by any means necessary.

"No, the question is what they are planning," Kyson corrected. Kyson was the level headed one. He wasn't about to back down from anything that came their way, but he was the most reasonable thinker.

"That's what we don't know," Carlisle joined in. Carlisle was gung ho to put a stop to the hate... only if it could be done without fighting other South Polers. He didn't want the rivalry with the Clauses to turn into an all-out civil war here in the South Pole.

"Have you heard anything yet, Lorelei?" Noah asked.

Lorelei was one of the sweetest people Noah knew. She owned her own beauty salon, and as a result she heard a lot of gossip, some of it actually useful. Lorelei was very passionate about the cause, but no way could she ever be involved in anything violent. Noah was just too protective of her to let it come to that. Whatever he had to do, he would protect her.

"No, I haven't heard anything lately," she admitted morosely, but even that couldn't stop the tinkling of her high pitched voice like bells on Christmas morning. Lorelei was such a tiny thing, she would be practically useless if and when it came to actual conflict. She was at least a foot shorter than Noah with a tiny build. She had light blonde hair that looked like corn silk... except brighter and softer. She had pale skin that almost seemed to glow.

"Maybe that means there is nothing at all going on, and Eddie is over reacting as usual," Milo suggested eagerly. What Milo wanted most was for everyone to forget about the feud and things to die down the way they had before Wynter or Mrs. Clause showed up. He wanted what he considered normal, but that would never happen.

Wynter had come to live at the South Pole, and Mrs. Clause had come looking for her daughter. They were the catalyst, and nothing would ever be the same again. A ball had started rolling that could never be stopped.

"No, I don't think he is," Declan responded. "Not this time. Something is definitely up. My family has been acting especially odd and racist lately. They're acting weird towards me."

"Mine too," Noah agreed.

"There's nothing new there," Stewart continued to argue. "Both of your families have practically disowned you, because you refuse to make a stand against the Clauses."

"At least we were man enough to stand up for what we believe. Our family knows how we feel about the feud. Does your family know how you feel?" Declan shot back at Stewart.

"That's not the point. The point is that there is nothing going on, and even if there was what are you going to do about it, huh?"

"Oh, that's right. You want to sit back and watch everyone tear each other limb from limb," Declan scoffed.

"That's a little extreme don't you think?" Owen inserted. "No one is really going to go that far."

"Aren't they? There is a lot of hate between the South Pole and the North Pole. You are surrounded by it all day, every day. You must realize that here in the South Pole people are ready for violence; they want to see the Clauses pay. The Clauses are fiercely outnumbered, but the South Pole is no match for the Clauses. It would be a massacre on both sides."

"It's true," Noah agreed. "Any one of the Clauses could stop an attack with a single flick of their wrist."

"Yeah? But how many could they stop at one time?" Enoch asked.

"I don't know, but come on. The man flies around the world in one night visiting children's houses. That's some powerful magic."

"What about the daughter? How powerful is her magic?" Kyson asked.

"She, uh, she's stronger than any of us," Noah answered reluctant to out Wynter.

Kyson quirked a brow at him and pushed, "You know her. You even saw her in her own environment last year. How strong is she?"

"Strong enough to take any of us."

Kyson burst into laughter bringing the interrogation to an end.

"Let's just keep our eyes and ears open until the next time we meet," Noah instructed, and the group dispersed.

"Can I walk you home?" Noah asked Lorelei.

"I'd like that... I'm sorry I wasn't more help back there."

"You've had more to add than any of us. Don't worry about anything that did or didn't happen tonight."

"Well, I'm going to keep my ears open," Lorelei promised.

"I would appreciate that. So, how are things going?" Noah asked.

"Oh, you know, about the same as always."

"Business is still going well?" Noah worried that her business would slack off as people realized she didn't feel the same as others about the Clauses.

"Business is good... I actually feel like I'm deceiving my customers," Lorelei admitted.

"How so?"

"I don't think any of them realize how I really feel about this whole feud with the Clauses. They never ask, so I don't tell anyone. I listen to what they say about the feud but never add my own two cents... I'm sort of scared that when they learn the truth, they won't want me doing their hair anymore."

"Yeah, I've wondered the same thing myself. I don't think it hurts anything to keep your feelings to yourself."

"You haven't kept yours to yourself."

"No, I haven't, but I haven't had much of a choice short of lying. I have been asked specifically about the situation repeatedly. No one has asked you, so you haven't lied."

"What happens if someone does ask me? I won't lie about it."

"Then you don't."

"But, once the truth comes out, my roommate is going to throw me out. I know she will, and if I lose all my business, I won't be able to afford another place. What will I do?"

"You could always come stay with me. I have an extra room, and I don't have a lot of friends around here to use the room."

"That is very generous of you, but I couldn't impose on you."

"You wouldn't be imposing."

"So, the girl is pretty strong, huh."

"Yeah. Yeah, she is."

"I heard you had a crush on her when you were younger."

"I did. I was just a kid, and she was my first crush."

"She's pretty?"

"She's beautiful inside and out. That's what makes what's going on so wrong. Wynter doesn't deserve this."

"Oh, yeah… You didn't say much about your trip last year. How was she doing?"

"Great, she was pregnant… very pregnant."

"Oh! Who is the father?"

"Anthony."

"Anthony Phillips? The vampire?"

"Yeah, they're great together."

"So, it was true? He really did leave to go find her?"

"Yeah, they sort of saved each other."

"Good, I-I mean that's good that they are happy."

"Yes, it is, and they deserve that happiness. What they don't deserve is hostility from the South Pole."

"They won't be able to escape it."

"No… I'm afraid not. I won't make them go it alone, though."

"Are you going to leave us?"

Noah took a deep breath and let it out slowly, stalling for time. "That's hard to answer. I'm not sure what the future of this feud will bring."

"What happens to us here if you leave?"

"I don't know. That's part of why I don't know if I'm leaving."

Lorelei studied her hands silently, yet her face was awash with a multitude of emotions, emotions that Noah couldn't read. He wished there was more time, but they were at Lorelei's apartment building.

"I'll see you later?" Noah asked nervously.

"Yeah, later."

Lorelei disappeared into her apartment, and Noah started the lonely trek to his own small cabin.

Chapter Four

"Do you really think I can do this?" Anthony asked as he and Wynter walked through the stables hand in hand.

"You? You've admired the man and the job for centuries. I can't think of anyone more fitting to take over for Daddy."

Blitzen was hopping around her stall as only the truly hyper can do. "Hey, girl, settle down," Anthony said and reached his free hand toward Blitzen.

Blitzen immediately settled and nuzzled Anthony's hand with her nose. It was amazing the things that Anthony could accomplish with Blitzen. No one else had the knack that Anthony did, not even Santa himself.

Anthony was great with all the reindeer; in fact, since having Noel took up so much more of Wynter's time, Anthony had been working more with the reindeer. He was trying to get Comet and Dasher moving about more and picking up the pace. The two laziest reindeer in the stable, Wynter wasn't sure if they would ever do any better.

"I've barely even set foot in the toy factory."

"That was your choice," Wynter pointed out.

"I just feel like a giant in there."

"Everyone feels like a giant compared to elves… The elves listen to you."

"I'm the largest creature at the North Pole after Roscoe. I would listen to me too if I were elf size."

Wynter stopped dead in her tracks and pulled her hand away from Anthony's in order to hold her middle as she doubled over with laughter. "You're exaggerating. You're not bigger than all the reindeer."

"You're hilarious," Anthony deadpanned.

"Do you think we should get back up to the house?"

"Probably. It was sweet of your mom to offer to watch Noel for a while, but she's been a handful lately."

Anthony was right. Noel had been a handful and then some. She had recently discovered her magic and was exploring through it. She was notorious for

levitating things to her from across the room then pitching them away again. Anthony and Wynter could only imagine the state of chaos her parents' house must be in by now.

"What if I'm not strong enough?" Anthony asked as they started back. "I'm not a blood born Clause, you know."

"That fact hasn't escaped me. You'll do just fine; now, stop worrying. I believe nature has a way of working everything out. The job of Santa has never gone to a female, and you're stronger than my mother ever was. Dad says that you're stronger than he remembers his mom being or even his grandmother. You're the strongest non-blood born Clause that anyone can remember. Besides if Daddy thinks you can do the job, you can do it. He wouldn't pass such an important job to someone who wasn't capable. He takes the job of Santa very seriously."

"I know. I just have so many doubts about taking over as Santa, you included."

"What's that supposed to mean?" Wynter asked in a shocked voice.

"Could we talk about it later?"

They had already reached the house, and Anthony was obviously uncomfortable talking about whatever was bothering him in front of Santa and Mrs. Clause. Wynter nodded and reluctantly let it go.

The door swung wide open reveling Santa with food across the front of his shirt and a big grin plastered across the front of his face. "Wynter! Noel is just like you! She behaves just like you did at this age," he laughed in his booming voice.

"So, I'm being punished for your past?" Anthony teased Wynter playfully.

"If she's paying me back now, I dread seeing what those frightful teen years will be like when she's paying you back."

"I was a rather well behaved teen," Anthony said with a thoughtful look. "It wasn't until my twenties that I really began to cause strife. That was when… Oh, between my own rebellious behavior and yours, we might do better to lock Noel up during her twenties."

"That would just cause her to rebel more," Wynter pointed out.

"Not all of our children's rebellions turn out that bad. It brought you here to us," Santa reminded Anthony.

"I guess you're right," Anthony said with a loving look at his wife.

"Well, this has been fun, but I've got to get back to the naughty and nice list. Care to join me Anthony?"

"Oh, um…" Anthony looked at Wynter as if nervously seeking approval.

"Go on. I've got this down here," Wynter assured him. What was going on with Anthony? He had never been so reluctant before. He had always valued Wynter's opinion about things, but he had never sought her approval before everything he did.

Wynter took Noel out of the high chair saying, "I think you've had enough, you little trouble maker. Did you get any of it in your mouth, or is it all on Papa?"

"Papa," Noel cooed and giggled.

"He spoils her, more than he did you at that age," Mom supplied, not that Wynter needed telling that her dad spoiled Noel. "I used to worry that we would never get you under control the way he spoiled you. But, he knew that you were our only child, and he didn't want to miss a single opportunity to dote on you."

"You knew when I was that young that you wouldn't have any other children?" Wynter asked surprised.

"Yeah," Mom nodded morosely. "I would have loved to have more kids, but it was a difficult pregnancy."

Wynter knew that her mom had a difficult pregnancy. She had heard those stories before, but she had never heard that it stopped them from having more children.

"You know how difficult the pregnancy was start to finish. What you don't know is how it affected your father. He almost didn't get everything done in time for Christmas Eve that year. He worried about me day and night, night and day. It scared him horribly. He honestly thought he was going to lose us both, and that was something he couldn't go through again. The night you were born, he told me that he couldn't stand to risk my life like that again, and he vowed that we wouldn't have any more kids."

Wynter sat Noel down to go play while she stood there for a few seconds in shock. "How have I not heard any of this before?"

"Your dad didn't think we should tell you."

"Why?"

"He didn't want you to think you hadn't been worth the risk or that you were unwanted. We love you very much, and we were overjoyed to have you. It just wasn't something your dad thought he could live through again, but you were always wanted."

Wynter hugged her mom without a sound then sprinted up the stairs and down the hall to her father's office. It was hard to think of her dad scared. She had never seen him scared of anything. All those years she had longed for a sibling, she had no idea it was because her dad was scared, and to think at one time she had actually believed that her parents chose to not to have more kids because of the disappointment she had been.

Inside the office, Wynter flung her arms around her father and hugged him tight. "I love you, Daddy," she whispered.

There were tears flowing down Wynter's cheeks as she stayed right there and held her dad close.

"Wynter, baby, is everything okay?" Anthony asked. Wynter could hear the concern in his voice, but she didn't spare him a look. "I thought I was a disappointment."

"Oh," Anthony mumbled. He had heard all that before.

"What are you talking about?" Santa asked.

"Mama told me everything. She told me why you didn't want any other children."

"Ah... Oh, my baby girl, come here." Santa turned and pulled Wynter into his lap. "You were never a disappointment. Rambunctious, stubborn, and rebellious but never a disappointment. The reason I didn't want more kids had nothing to do with you. I love you so much."

"I love you too, Daddy."

Anthony quietly excused himself to give Wynter some time alone with her dad. It was about time they had this conversation. It was a long time overdue.

He slipped downstairs and helped Mrs. Clause finish cleaning up.

"I'm sorry you ever thought that, Wynter."

"It was part of why I went to the South Pole, and I'm not sorry I went to the South Pole. That's where I found Anthony."

"Yeah, and that polite young man. What was his name?"

"Noah," Wynter supplied.

"That was him. I liked him."

"Noah is from the South Pole."

"I was just as surprised as you," Daddy admitted. "I was scared when I couldn't find you, but you might be right. Your time at the South Pole might not have been all bad. You brought a lot back with you. Besides Noah and Anthony, who led to my beautiful granddaughter, you brought back a tolerance and understanding that no Clause before you possessed."

"What about you, Daddy? You brought Noah to the North Pole."

"I did do that. I did that for you. There's not much I wouldn't do for my baby girl, and any tolerance and understanding I show is because of what my baby girl brought me."

"Anthony says that some prejudices go too deep. He doesn't believe that the North and South Poles will ever get along. What do you think?"

"Well... I don't know if we'll ever be great friends, but I do believe that if anyone can teach us all some tolerance, it's you."

Chapter Five

"Merry Christmas!" Noah's mom greeted Christmas morning.

"Merry Christmas, Mom."

"Glad you made it," Ethan said.

"Where else would I be on Christmas?" Noah returned.

"The North Pole maybe."

"That's enough," Dad intervened. "No talk of the North Pole today. It stresses your mother."

Noah knew it stressed his mother to see them constantly fighting. He also knew it enraged his father as much as it did Ethan for Noah to side with Wynter. Dad played the part of the peacemaker until the topic came around to Wynter Clause.

"It won't matter much longer anyway," Ethan mumbled under his breath.

"Ethan, I said that was enough," Dad grimaced.

"No, I want to hear this. What was that supposed to mean? What won't matter?"

"None of it will matter when the Clauses are taken care of."

"Taken care of? What are you going to do, Ethan? Are you going to hurt Wynter? She was like a sister to us."

"To you maybe."

"No, Ethan, to us! There was a time when you cared for her too. She was your friend back before you knew her last name was Clause. You loved her once. Love isn't based on a name. A true friend doesn't care what your name is. The question is what kind of friend are you?"

"What kind of friend was she? She knew the score when she came here. What you should be asking yourself is what she was doing here in the first place."

"Why don't we go ask her then?"

"Are you suicidal, little brother? The Clauses would just as soon kill you as hear you out."

"Wynter never hurt anyone while she was down here."

"That may be so, but she's back home with mommy and daddy now."

"So, you admit that Wynter isn't the enemy?" Noah challenged.

"She lied to all of us."

"Look all around you! Look at yourself, Ethan! If she had introduced herself as a Clause, she would have been immediately imprisoned or worse! I would have lied in her position too."

"I hope I raised you better than to ever put yourself in that sort of situation," Mom lectured. "Now, let's talk about something more pleasant. Noah, how's work?"

Well, that settled that. They were definitely planning something. Noah just had no idea what. Yet.

"Work's great, Mom. We're busy. The humans are getting more and more curious every day."

"Oh my! Could you imagine if they do find us? We'd have to hide who we really are. I don't even want to think about how hard that would be."

Wynter could tell them exactly how hard it is to hide your true nature, but no one wanted to hear that.

"We won't let that happen," Noah assured her. Surrounded by rangers the South Pole was protected from ever having to hide who they really are, yet Wynter was on her own with no one to rely on but herself.

"That's nice. Would you set the table for me?"

"Sure." Noah started pulling plates from the cabinet while Ethan and his dad left the kitchen huddled together and talking in hushed tones. Now would be the perfect time to find out what they were up to, but his mom had him effectively distracted for now.

Lunch was delicious, and there was no more talk of Wynter or the North Pole. For a while things felt like the good old days before their world had become consumed with hate.

"You must have been hungry," Mom laughed watching Noah load his plate up with a second heaping helping of ham.

"What can I say? I'm a growing boy."

"Hardly," Dad joined in the laughter.

"If you play hard, you've got to eat hard, right, Noah?" Ethan offered. "Yeah, it looks like he's been spending so much time with the animals, he's beginning to eat like one."

"Oh, speaking of animals, your dad tells me you've been working with rabbits?" Mom wanted to know.

"Not rabbits, Mom, arctic hares."

"Aren't they the same thing?"

"Not exactly."

"But, I bet they're cute and a lot safer than a lot of the animals you've worked with before."

"They are very cute. You would love them."

"Maybe you could take a picture for me?"

"I can't risk scaring them off with a camera or even my phone. I'd have to have someone hiding nearby to take the picture." Someone like Wynter was the part Noah left unsaid.

"That would be a good job for someone, and I know we have plenty of young people right now looking for a job," Dad added.

Sure, there were a couple dozen young people currently looking for a job, but none of them had the same talent for photography as Wynter. Wynter had a knack for catching the very essence of a moment in all its tenderness, fierceness, and emotional reaches. She was able to capture things that Noah himself hadn't even noticed in the thrill of the moment. For instance, in his

favorite picture she took of him feeding a seal, the first thing he noticed was the ferociousness of the seal with his mouth opened wide, showing of long sharp teeth. Noah didn't notice until later that if you looked closely there was a polar bear standing off in the not too far distance watching the whole scene unfurl.

It wasn't until much later that he learned the identity of that very special polar bear was none other than Wynter's pet, Roscoe. There was so many more watching Noah's back that day than he had known. He knew that Wynter and Ethan stood behind him, Ethan with shotgun in hand. What he hadn't known was the power that Wynter wielded or that the nearby Roscoe would also have charged in to help any friend of Wynter.

"Maybe it would," Noah indulged them.

"The rangers could hold tryouts," Ethan suggested with a big teasing grin.

"Right, I'll get right on that," Noah laughed along.

"Finish up," Mom instructed. "We'll open gifts when you're all finished."

They were nearly finished opening gifts when the doorbell rang. "Now, who could that be on Christmas Day?" Mom wondered aloud.

Everyone got up and went together to the door, but when they opened the door a delivery man stood waiting with a long, wide, flat package. "I've got a package for Noah."

"On Christmas Day?"

"Special delivery."

"And, they make you work on Christmas!?!" Mom exclaimed.

"I just do as I'm told. Have a merry Christmas!" With that the delivery man returned to his sled and left.

"Noah?" Dad said handing the package to Noah. "There's no return address."

"Well, open it up," Ethan urged.

"That's terrible that they make that poor man work on Christmas Day," Mom continued to fret.

Noah tore into the package and found a framed picture waiting inside. It was a picture of an adorable little girl riding on the back of a very familiar polar bear. The little girl had dark ringlet curls against a pale complexion that one could only acquire living in either the extreme north or the extreme south. She had big, round eyes that were nearly as black as coal. She had merry little dimples set deep into her cheeks outlining a truly precious smile.

"What an adorable little girl!" Mom exclaimed.

"She seems to be the spitting image of a certain vampire you were fascinated with as a preteen," Ethan accused. "Who would be sending you a photo of a little girl the spitting image of Anthony?"

"Do you think she looks like him?" Noah replied vaguely. "I don't remember Anthony having dimples so cute. As a matter of fact, I don't remember him having dimples at all."

"No, I don't think he did… How did that old poem about Santa Clause go? 'His dimples how merry'? A Clause trait then I suppose. Interesting, isn't it? A child the spitting image of Anthony bearing Clause traits."

"Noah," Mom said in her warning tone.

"Oh, come on, Mom. You're not buying this, are you? How many millions of people around the world have dimples? It's not an exclusively Clause trait; neither is dark hair and eyes exclusive to Anthony's lineage. I have never laid eyes on this little girl before, and if Ethan has he should speak up now to tell me where he met such an adorable child or where this photo came from."

"Ethan?" Dad questioned.

"I've never seen her," Ethan admitted with a defeated tone.

The girl must have been almost a year now. Noah turned the framed photo this way and that looking for a name, but there was none to be found. He understood how dangerous it could be to plaster their daughter's name across anything in the South Pole, but Noah so longed to know what Anthony and Wynter had named their little girl.

Later that night, Noah invited his two best friends and Lorelei over for a Christmas nightcap.

Chapter Six

"Hey, how was your trip?" Wynter asked kissing an exhausted looking Anthony on the cheek.

Immediately Anthony's face lit up, and a broad smile overtook the look of exhaustion. "It was amazing! Oh, and the cookies. There were so many cookies, millions of cookies, and no one telling you when you've had enough."

"I'm sure you never got tired of them either."

"Of course not. I love cookies!"

"I know you do."

"It wasn't just the cookies either. Santa just flowed through the whole night like a well oiled machine. Do you have any idea how much planning and organization goes into his Christmas Eve flight? Obviously his route is planned, but the toys are organized in his bag in coordination with the route plan."

"I have an idea how much prep work it takes."

"I'm sorry, Wynter, but wow. The magic that it takes is intense! He throws magic around like you do, like it is completely natural."

"It is natural for us and anyone else who was born with it," Wynter pointed out.

"Not like this. Your mother doesn't throw magic around like this. No one in the South Pole threw magic around like this."

"You know the people from the South Pole don't have that kind of magic to be throwing around, and Mom isn't a blood born Clause."

"Neither am I. What if I can't wield that much magic? I mean, how do we know it shouldn't be you taking over instead?"

"Are we back to this again?" Wynter sighed with exasperation. "There has never been a female Santa Clause, and there never will be. That is not the way this works. You just have to believe."

"It's hard to believe I'll ever have that much magic."

"You believed in Santa for centuries. Not many adults still believe, but you actually wrote letters to Santa as an adult."

"That was easier to believe. After I was turned, it wasn't a far stretch to believe Santa existed too."

"You believed in me."

"I could see you with my own eyes. I could reach out and touch you." Anthony took both Wynter's hands and pulled their bodies flush together. "There was no denying that you are very real."

"You automatically believed I was a Clause."

"I saw the way you threw magic around even then."

"Everyone else believed I was from the South Pole. I could have been an anomaly, couldn't I? You never asked if I was Santa's daughter or if I was even a Clause. You simply believed. Do that again."

"But, Wynter–"

"No, but's. Besides, I don't want the job, never did."

"Yeah, that still bothers me too. I don't want Noel running away the way you did."

"It didn't turn out that bad for us."

"No, it didn't," Anthony smiled still holding Wynter tight, "but the pain that drove you away was real. I don't want Noel to ever feel that."

"You are not my father. That isn't going to happen. We won't let it, and we'll do it all with you in the role of Santa."

"You seem so sure."

"I am."

"You promise everything will work out? I don't want my family to suffer."

"Everything will work out exactly the way it's supposed to."

"Good, because I really want to do this."

Wynter laughed at Anthony's enthusiasm that couldn't be crushed by any amount of worry. "Go get some rest. You look tired."

"Noel will be getting up soon. I'll wait."

"Don't set precedents now that you can't possibly keep up with. Noel will be fine. You go get some sleep. Noel and I will be fine for a few hours, and when you wake up we'll do our Christmas."

"Are you sure?"

"Yes."

"I love you." Anthony kissed Wynter and went to bed. It wasn't a quick kiss from the weary either. It was a kiss full of the elation Anthony had felt playing Santa.

Wynter smiled. Her husband was in so many ways still a wide eyed child full of wonder. She couldn't think of anyone better for the job of Santa. The world would be lucky to have a Santa who still sees the job as privilege rather than a family duty.

She went to work cooking a large brunch. She knew that Anthony would be hungry when he woke up, and he was going to need something more substantial than the cookies he so loved.

Noel only slept for thirty minutes after Anthony got home. Afraid that Noel would start tearing into the gifts in the living room, Wynter put up an invisible barrier to keep Noel in the kitchen.

Wynter had been so touched by Anthony's insistence that he put out Noel's gifts rather than Daddy. Tonight was supposed to be a ride along. Anthony was not responsible for anything but observing, but that didn't stop him from doing his own home all on his own. He set each gift out carefully arranged before he left to meet Santa for their long night.

He wouldn't always be able to do his own home first. As Noel got older, the later she'd stay up, and the harder it would be to start at home. Then again it wasn't as if the identity of Santa would ever be a secret from Noel.

"Wynter?" Mom called from the back door.

"Hey, Merry Christmas!"

"Merry Christmas, sweetheart. So, how did Anthony think it went?"

"He was so excited, I don't know how he ever got to sleep."

"That's basically what your father said too. I think tonight was a relief to him."

"A relief?" Wynter questioned.

"You father started worrying about retirement the day you turned eighteen."

"What?"

"Yeah, he worried that we had sheltered you too much. He was worried you may never leave the North Pole to marry or that it might take you decades."

"How ridiculous," Wynter cackled.

"That's why we tried to give you space when you left... for a while, but when your father couldn't find you

we panicked." A tear slipped down Mom's cheek. "For a horrible two days we thought you were gone. The South Pole didn't occur to us as a possibility for so long. We were so overjoyed to finally figure out you weren't dead... Your father wanted to run right out after you, but he was in a frightened rage. I was afraid he would kill anyone who stood between him and getting to you."

"Is that not what you threatened? What you almost did with that fireball?"

"No, no, I threatened, yes, but it was nothing but words. I could feel you nearby but couldn't find you. I knew you wouldn't let the fireball do any damage. It wasn't strong anyway. Your father was so mad when I made him wait here."

"I-I thought he was too busy to come," Wynter admitted.

"What? Oh, Wynter, he called a halt to everything when he thought you were dead. He only got things started up again when I went after you because he needed to keep himself distracted."

"Gam, Gam, Gam!" Noel squealed and plowed into Mrs. Clause's legs.

"Merry Christmas to you too, precious," she said picking up Noel and kissing her little cheek.

"Cookie, Gam!"

"I don't know. It may be too early for cookies," Mrs. Clause said looking to Wynter for clearance.

"You have Cheerios and orange slices. Eat them," Wynter said.

"No orange. Cookie," Noel screeched.

"On that note I'm going to excuse myself," Mrs. Clause said, handing Noel off to Wynter. "We will come down when your father gets up."

"Bye, Mom. Noel, no." Wynter sat Noel down at her child sized table and chairs that the elves had made especially for Noel. "You can eat Cheerios, or you can wait for Daddy."

"Daddy, Daddy, Daddy," Noel screamed.

"Shh, let Daddy sleep. He worked hard last night."

"Daddy, cookie."

"Mmm, we'll see."

Anthony slept for no more than four hours before he was up and excited to spend Christmas Day with his young family. By that time Noel had forgotten all about

cookies, because she was more interested in Daddy throwing her up in the air and catching her.

"What are you up to, kiddo? Have you been driving Mommy crazy while you waited for that lazy Daddy of yours to get out of bed?"

"Daddy!" Noel giggled.

"Something sure smells good. What were you and Mommy cooking?"

"Breakfast!"

"Good, I'm starving."

"I don't see how you could be after all those c-o-o-k-i-e-s," Wynter spelled out.

"Hollow leg is the trick. I empty my stomach completely every couple hours, so I'm overdue," Anthony smiled.

Wynter loved his charming smile. "I almost believe you."

"Let's eat."

Wynter ate a plate full of fruit and breakfast casserole and did her best to get Noel to eat something substantial enough to stay with her through the morning's excitement, because she knew that food was the last thing Noel would be interested in after all the excitement started.

"Mmm, that was delicious, Wynter," Anthony complimented.

"Delicious, Mommy," echoed Noel, who had been in a copying phase as of late.

"Well, thank you both. Are we ready to go to the living room to see what Santa left?" Wynter asked with a warm smile for her husband.

"Papa!" Noel called and looked toward the living room clearly expecting her papa to be waiting in the next room.

"No, not yet," Wynter corrected gently.

"Come on, beautiful. Let's go take a look," Anthony said lifting Noel.

He carried her into the living room and sat down on the couch with her, and Wynter sat down next to him and snuggled into his side. Anthony took his Bible from the end table and read from Luke about the very first Christmas the same as he had done last year. It had become their own Christmas tradition. Wynter watched the way his facial expression changed. He used added

emphasis and eccentrics to keep Noel's attention. He was so good with her.

Chapter Seven

"How was your Christmas?" Kyson asked as he fixed an eggnog for himself and Lorelei.

Noah sipped on his spiced cider while he pondered the answer and almost choked on the stout liquor Declan had used. Declan certainly liked his strong, and no one could deny that. "We've had worse," Noah finally answered. "We actually got along for the better part of the day."

"That's an improvement."

"Guess so... Eddie was right. There is something going on."

"Never said he was wrong."

"Ethan actually told me that the Clause's were going to be taken care of."

"Sounds serious. So, what are we going to do?" Declan asked.

"I don't know... I got a package from Wynter today."

"At your parents' house?" Lorelei asked horrified.

"Yep," Noah answered with an amused smirk.

"Yeah? What was it?" Declan wanted to know.

"A picture of their little girl. I played it off like I didn't know who the kid was or who it was from, but there's no mistaking it. She looks too much like Anthony."

Declan and Kyson both burst out in raucous laughter.

Lorelei jumped to her feet nearly spilling her eggnog. "Oh, I've never seen any of the Clauses myself! You have to show me the picture! Please."

Noah led her into the bedroom where he had left the picture laying on the bed.

"Oh, Noah! She's so adorable. Look at those dimples. Does Wynter have dimples like that?"

"Nah, but I'm like Ethan on that one; I assume it's a Clause trait."

Lorelei gasped, "He knew?"

"They all knew. Mom tried to pretend like she didn't. Just like everything else, she thought if she ignored it, then it would cease to exist."

"What'd Ethan do?"

"Blew his top. I pointed out that dimples aren't an uncommon trait and that the little girl could be anyone. The picture could have come from anywhere. I asked him if he knew where it came from, turned it on him so that Mom was questioning him instead of me. That got the whole thing dropped real quick."

"That polar looks so real too."

"Man, that polar is real," Declan said from behind them.

"Yeah, it is," Noah agreed. "That's Roscoe. That was another reason I knew who the little girl was."

"No way! That is the bear? That's Roscoe?"

"Yeah."

"Move over," Kyson ordered pushing Declan out of the way. "How old is that kid?"

"She'd be almost a year by now."

"One year, and riding on the back of a polar bear like it's some big dog or something? Those Clause's do have some serious magic and maybe born without fear."

"Sounds like the three of you?" Lorelei compared.

"Hardly," Kyson laughed, "although that might be true of Noah here."

"Yeah, a man has to be fearless to ride all the way to the North Pole with Santa himself," Declan added.

"I have just as many fears as you do. It's just my fears are concentrated in different areas."

"Well, I just added a new fear to my list of fears," Lorelei interjected. "What's going to happen to this adorable little girl if a war breaks out between the North and the South?"

All four of them stared at the little girl in the picture with horrible possibilities rolling around in their minds.

"That's a good question," Noah sighed.

Kyson clapped a large hand on Noah's shoulder. "So, what is it you fear?"

"I fear protecting all the people I love on both sides of a war."

The four friends stayed quiet for a time later just watching the picture as if the bear and little girl in the picture might start moving about. The wind blew outside making a whistling sound. The snow was quietly falling to the ground while sleet pinged off the side of the house. Even the silence seemed loud.

"What are we going to do?" Lorelei asked.

"I don't know," Noah hated to admit.

"I know one thing," Kyson started. "The odds aren't good. There are only thirteen of us like-minded people. Of those thirteen only seven of us are even willing to make a stand. Of those seven how many are going to do any good when things start getting violent?"

"Eddie sure won't do anyone any good," Declan laughed.

"I wouldn't mind seeing Vivienne teaching a few lessons," Kyson grinned.

"You got a thing for Vivienne?" Lorelei asked.

"Tough as nails. Attitude to spare. Long shapely athletic build. Hair like a raven. What's not to love?"

Everyone got a kick out of that, and it managed to loosen the mood.

Over the next couple weeks, everyone in their ragtag rebel group gathered intel. Ironically enough it was the ones who absolutely didn't want conflict who gathered the most intel. It was probably because none of them had ever let their true feelings about the feud be known.

Blossom and Stewart were arguing when Noah walked into their next meeting.

"You know it's true," Blossom insisted vehemently.

"What I know is that people talk. They shoot off at the mouth, especially when they're emotional," Stewart rebuffed.

Noah gave Kyson a questioning look, but Kyson just shrugged and looked to Declan.

Declan shook his head and tried to explain. "It seems that Blossom and Stewart have heard the same exact thing, yet they have two very different interpretations."

"Go on. Tell him what you found out," Eddie pushed them.

"A bunch of guys are planning an expedition to the North Pole. They're going to kill Santa," Blossom said.

"They'll never get past the magical wards to Santa," Noah countered.

"Exactly," Stewart exploded. "They know that too. That's how I know they're just shooting off at the mouth."

"No, they weren't. You heard them. They were dead serious. I don't know how they plan to do it, but they believe they've found a way around the magical wards," Blossom continued to argue.

"But, that's impossible. I mean, isn't it?" Lorelei asked looking to Noah for the answer.

"Yes," Noah answered firmly. "Our magic is no match for theirs. There's no way that any South Poler is getting past those wards."

"Well, the point is they think so at least, and they plan to go up there and do something about it," Blossom said.

"When?" Declan asked.

"In one month."

"A month?"

Blossom nodded.

"Why so soon?" Enoch asked. "Sure, they have the element of surprise, but waiting longer would give them more time to prepare."

"How long have they been preparing, do you think?" Eddie asked nervously, but then everything about conflict made Eddie nervous.

"Haven't you thought for a while that they were up to something?" Enoch asked. "Maybe they've been planning this from the very day after Mrs. Clause left. They might be well prepared and have already figured out exactly how to get past the magical wards protecting the Clauses."

"Do you have to do that?" Blossom asked desperately. "You make it sound so violent."

"It is violent. That's the very nature of war, and this is a war. Don't kid yourself. The only question is which side is more prepared. Are the Clauses so powerful that they are impenetrable, or are the Clauses so comfortable in their arrogance that they set themselves up for attack."

"You sound like the rest of them now, talking about the Clause arrogance," Owen accused.

"I would be arrogant too if I had that kind of magic," Enoch said.

"This is ridiculous," Milo gripped. "I mean, what are they really going to do, and what can we actually do about it?"

"There's a lot we can do about it, actually, if we have the guts to try," Declan responded.

"What do you mean? What do you think we can do?" Carlisle wanted to know.

"A lot," Vivienne answered for Declan. "Are you with us or not?"

"What does that mean? You want to fight against your friends and family?" Everett asked.

"If it comes to that then I won't back down from doing the right thing, and you know this is the right thing. What has Santa ever done to any of you?" Vivienne challenged. "He does so much for the human children, but he's never hurt us."

"So, you'll take his side over your own family?" Owen returned the challenge.

"No, but you know this is wrong."

"What I know is that I have no reason to hate the Clauses. Maybe my parents do. I don't know, but I won't hurt my parents over a difference of opinion."

"No one is talking about hurting our family," Kyson offered.

"And, you believe that? What about the rest of you? Do you believe that? Noah? Are you prepared to hurt your parents or Ethan?"

"Of course not, but I also know that neither is Wynter."

"What if they are attacking her?" Carlisle probed. "Will she still be so forgiving then?"

"Yes. You don't know her like I do. She loves them. She could never hurt them."

"What if they become a threat to her family?" Enoch questioned.

"That's cute. Whose side are you on, Enoch?" Vivienne demanded.

"Same side you are, but if things get ugly we need to be prepared for every eventuality. So, how about it? What if they become a threat to her family?"

"I don't know. I'm sure she'll protect her family, but the thing is she sees my family as family too," Noah tried to explain.

"That's likely something she couldn't answer herself right now," Kyson jumped in to help.

Enoch nodded thoughtfully but let it go.

"So, that brings us back to, what are we going to do?" Declan asked again.

"I think the first thing we need to do is define what's going on here," Vivienne decided. "If they attack Santa, then the Clauses will see that as an act of war. There will be no other way to see it. That attack is as good as declaring war. From the second they start their attack the South Pole is at war with the North Pole... Everyone here is going to have to choose a side once and for all."

"No way," Owen burst out. "I'm like Switzerland. I'm completely neutral in this whole thing."

Everyone turned expectantly to Noah, who sighed and said, "Then you've chosen your side."

"What is that supposed to mean?" Owen replied.

"If you won't help us stop this, then you are no better than the ones who are instigating it. Vivienne was right it is time to choose your side."

"So, you are going to go fight with the Clauses like they're going to make you an honorary North Poler?" Stewart accused.

"I'm going to fight to stop all of this nonsense, and I can guarantee that is exactly what Wynter Clause wants as well... It's time to choose your side, and if you choose to remain neutral, you might as well quit wasting your time with these meetings… We'll go around the room and let everyone declare themselves."

"In front of everyone?" Milo asked indignantly.

"If you can't declare your side in front of us, then you're a coward who would never declare anything in front of others. That leaves you on their side," Declan said quickly getting fired up.

"Oh yeah, who's side are you on? Will you fight for the North Pole?"

"I will," declared Declan.

"So, will I," Kyson declared. Kyson turned to look to the person to his left indicating that they should declare themselves next.

Enoch sitting to Kyson's left didn't even flinch. He declared, "I will fight for the North Pole." Enoch looked to Blossom on his left.

Blossom shook her head as a tear rolled down her face. "I can't do it. I can't fight. I'm out." Then she stood and fled from the room.

All eyes in the room turned to Noah who had been sitting to Blossom's left. "I think you all know where I stand. I will fight for the North Pole."

Eddie was next. "I-I'm on your side."

"Not a chance. I'm not fighting," Stewart declared.

Lorelei looked up with a trembling lip. Noah so wished he could scare away everything that scared her and stop that trembling lip. Maybe more than that he wished he could kiss that tremble away and hold her until all the fear just fell away.

"I will fight for the North Pole," she said in a shaky whisper.

Noah swallowed the lump in his throat. Lorelei was so scared but still agreed to fight. That made her declaration perhaps the bravest of them all.

They skipped over Declan who had already made his declaration and moved to Milo who said, "Leave me out of this."

Owen had already made himself perfectly clear, and Vivienne sat mute to his left.

"Vivienne?" Noah questioned.

"I'm in."

Noah caught the flinch on Kyson's face that he tried to cover. His face was a mask of confusion, and Noah made a mental note to check with him later.

Everett was quick to declare, "I'm out."

"Me too," Carlisle sighed. "I can't fight my own family."

Noah gave a nod and told, "Everyone keep your eyes and ears open. We need to find out when they're planning the attack."

Chapter Eight

"Do you remember the first time you took a tour of the toy factory?" Anthony asked and kissed Wynter hello.

"Ah, no. It's just always been a part of my life. Why?"

He lay Noel, exhausted and sleeping, into her pack and play. "I was just thinking about today. It was Noel's first tour of the toy factory. I was curious if she would even remember it."

"She's one, Anthony. She's not going to remember."

"That's a shame. She really had a lot of fun today. You should have seen them all. You know how excited all the elves get over seeing her. They were like kids in a candy shop to have her in the toy factory today. I really think she believes they are life size toys themselves or maybe playmates, because they aren't much bigger than her. I don't guess they had seen her magic until today.

They were so enthralled. You would think she were the first Clause child to perform magic in the North Pole."

"What did she do?"

"She threw a trike across the room."

"She didn't!" Wynter gasped.

"Oh yeah. What made it worse was that the elves were cheering so loudly she couldn't hear me get on to her. When I tried again, your dad stopped me."

"And you listened to him? Daddy thinks Noel can do no wrong!"

"I know. It wouldn't have made a difference anyway. By that point the elves were all gathered around her oohing and aahing over her. The rest of the day they told her things to get for them. It was like having a dog play fetch, and Noel ate it up. She giggled until she coughed. She was more interested in playing magical games with the elves than she was the toys all around her."

"Like giving a child a new toy and watching them play with the box, huh?"

"Yeah, something like that. I suppose it gave the elves a well deserved break too."

"I'm sure. What did you think about the factory?"

"It was like the epitome of organization at its finest. It has been only weeks since Christmas, and the elves are already hard at work."

"It takes a long time to make that many toys," Wynter pointed out.

"I know. It's just… wow. The whole set up is amazing. Everything works together like a well oiled machine. It's exhausting work."

"I wouldn't know."

"I'm sorry, Wynter," Anthony said sympathetically as he pulled Wynter into his arms. "I promise that I'm always going to have time for you. What did you do today?"

"I wasn't accusing you of anything," Wynter chuckled. "I believe you when you say you'll always have time for us. It is actually kind of nice having you working with Dad. Mom and I had a girl's day. Look," Wynter urged thrusting her hand in front of Anthony's face. "We did each other's nails. I can't remember the last time that Mom had time for a girl's day. It was so much fun!"

"I'm glad you had fun. Is there anything to eat? I'm starving."

Wynter chuckled. "You're always hungry. Supper's not ready yet, but there are some cookies in the jar if you're interested."

"I'm always interested in cookies."

As Anthony opened the cookie jar and started helping himself to the cookies, Wynter stirred the chili that she had just set to simmer on the stove. "So, how did today go for you? Did you learn a lot?"

"Honestly? All I really learned is that I have a lot to learn. This is a huge operation."

"That's what happens when you have one family running an entire global operation. Did Dad hit you with too much too fast?"

"No… he didn't hit with anything not really, yet he hit me with everything."

"Well, that's not cryptic. Explain please."

"Today he just gave me the grand tour. I got an overview of everything, but he didn't try to overwhelm with details. He said we had a year, he'd give me the details slowly. We're going to take it one aspect at a time."

"That sounds better."

"Yes, it does."

Over the next three weeks Anthony spent every day eight to five with Santa. He was dragging each day by the time he returned. Most days he left Noel at home with Wynter, but some of the easier or more fun days he would bring Noel along so that he and Santa could still spend time with her.

Today they were going to be outside with the reindeer for his first riding lesson. Santa had warned Anthony that it would take time to actually get up in the air. Anthony had planned to bring both Noel and Roscoe out to the reindeer stables… at least until he shared his plan with Wynter.

"Oh, I want to go to! That would be so much fun to spend the day with the reindeer. I stay so busy with Noel and housekeeping these days that I don't get to spend near as much time with them as I used to. Teaching you to drive the sleigh would be a perfect excuse to go out there."

"I'm sure you dad would like that to."

"Wynter!" Santa screamed as he barged into the house.

"Dad? Quit screaming. You're going to wake Noel."

"Santa, what are you doing here? We're not supposed to meet for another two hours."

"Just look at this letter I got!" Santa huffed out of breath.

Wynter took the letter from her dad's hand and held it between herself and Anthony.

Dear Santa,

I'm sorry to send such bad news by letter, but I really didn't know any other way to get in touch. I don't have any details yet like how many or when, but I know that there are plans being made to attempt an attack on you.

I didn't know what to do without more details, but I knew I had to give you a heads up incase I'm already too late. I'll write again when I have more details.

Noah

P.S. Tell Wynter and Anthony I said hi.

"An attack?" Wynter breathed.

"Things must be escalating down there," Anthony commented.

"Who would want to attack, though? Things have been stagnant for generations," Wynter pointed out.

"Things were stagnant until you made your escape to the South Pole. They felt deceived, like your presence had been a slap in the face. There are a lot down there that I wouldn't put it past them to attack if given half the chance. There are many, also, who saw your mother's visit to find you was an act of aggression. They would see an attack on the Clauses, on our family, as a retaliation," Anthony explained.

"You've been here for more than six years now. I'm sure things have only festered since you were there last," Santa pointed out.

"What are we going to do?" Wynter asked worry seeping into her voice.

"We're going to keep our eyes open and be cautious. The magical wards are still up. It's unlikely that they will get to us, but I still want everyone to be on alert," Santa said.

"How hard can it be to get through the magical wards?" Anthony questioned. "I got through."

"You're not from the South Pole or human," Santa replied.

"But, I was still a vampire at that time. Shouldn't the wards have kept me out?"

"No," Santa answered, "but that may be something to think about. The wards were never meant to keep out vampires. I don't think anyone ever dreamed that a vampire would be suicidal enough to come to us."

"Maybe I should go somewhere with Noel so that she's not in any danger," Wynter suggested.

"Not without me," Anthony nearly growled. "We can put my lessons on hold."

"No. I've worked hard too many years to let the South Pole come between me and my retirement," Santa gruffed. "Things should be just fine, but I'll call Mary just to be on the safe side... perhaps the others."

"Aunt Mary?" Wynter knew from talking to Anthony that her Aunt Mary was a vampire hunter, but she still had trouble picturing her sweet Aunt Mary in that role.

"Santa?"

"Yes, Anthony?"

"There's some bad blood between Mary and me."

"Oh, I wouldn't worry about that. I'm sure she put that all behind her at the w-... No, that's right. She wasn't able to make it back for the wedding. That almost killed her. She's always been so fond of Wynter. She never had any kids of her own."

"I'm well aware of that."

"No," Santa moaned as recognition dictated the features on his face. "Anthony, tell me you didn't have anything to do with Timothy."

Santa was practically begging, and Wynter had no idea what was going on anymore. "Who is Timothy?"

"Timothy was before your time, before you were even a twinkle in your mother's eye," Santa answered.

"I did not have anything to do with his murder, no, but that was during a particularly desperate time in my life… I did feed from his corpse."

"Oh, Anthony, this is going to make things harder. Still I think I should put in a few phone calls. Let's postpone the riding lesson," Santa said and hurried out of the house as quickly as he entered.

"Anthony? Tell me about Timothy and who he was to my Aunt Mary?" Wynter requested.

Anthony sighed deeply as if the memory alone pained him. He pulled out a dining chair and dropped into it. "It wasn't my first run in with Mary. My face was no more unfamiliar to her than hers was to me. I had already been struggling for years with what I had become and what I could do about it… I was so hungry all the

time… Just the thought of drinking blood was revolting, but when hunger pains become overwhelming, even the strongest man caves. I was still trying to figure out where I belonged in the world during those days, and I had fallen in with a less than desirable crowd. They were blood thirsty and unapologetic. They actually enjoyed the kill… I couldn't stand the loneliness of solitude back then. I had naively convinced myself that as long as I did not participate in their… less savory activities that their sin didn't touch me… I was stupid. I knew what they were doing, yet I stood back and let them do it. I was no better than them. I was just as guilty in my lack of action.

"Night after night they killed. I tried to keep my distance from the carnage, but the scent of blood was so strong. The hungrier I got, the more acutely aware I became of the scent. It became harder to ignore. My mouth watered even as my stomach churned. I yearned to join them in their disgusting feast. Somehow I resisted.

"I could only resist it for so long though. As time passed my stomach hurt. The pain worsened. I can remember lying on the ground moaning in pain as the others fed, but still it only worsened. My stomach distended, and I was sick all the time. Eventually instincts took over.

"One night I remember the pain and the smell of blood. That was when I lost control. I stood and started toward the scent. I was fully aware of what I was doing, yet it was like I was being controlled by some outside force. Out back the others were gathered around a bloodied body. There was no pulse left, no life. The man was already dead. I was not his murderer. There was nothing I could do to save him. I took solace in that fact, believing that what I did next was forgivable.

"I bent over the man and sunk my fangs deep. The blood was still hot, thick. The tang of iron was sharp. I remember thinking about how horrible the taste was and how sad it was that this was what my life had been reduced to. It didn't stop me from drinking though.

"Next, a loud, tormented scream ripped through the night. I looked up and was staring into the face of Mary Clause. There was no forgiveness on her face nor did I deserve it. I knew in that moment that I was every bit as guilty of that man's murder as the ones who had stopped his heart from beating. Mary knew it too.

"I'll never get the sound of her anguished cry out of my head or the look of agony on her face. We had taken everything from her. I didn't want to be a part of something so cruel, but I knew deep down that I was.

"She ran to his side, screaming his name, and we all scattered. It wasn't until later that I learned that man had been her fiancé, Timothy. Mary vowed her revenge. One by one she killed off the others, but by then I had distanced myself. I was already acclimating myself to solitude deciding that it would be best for everyone.

"I mourned for all the innocents who were killed mercilessly to appease our demonic appetites but none more than Timothy. I had seen the desperate grief on Mary's face that night, and I knew there was nothing that I could ever do to make up for that night. I'm the only one left alive from that night. Mary has hunted me from one end of the globe to the next."

"Does she know?"

"Know what? That I'm the one you married?"

Wynter nodded.

"I don't know, but I tend to believe she does not. None of your other aunts or uncles ever got close enough to me to recognize my face from before. Mary, however, is intimately familiar with my face but probably not my name."

"How do you think she will react?"

"Before or after trying to kill me?"

"Oh, Anthony!"

"We'll deal with it when she gets here, but your father is right to call in reinforcements."

"I've never seen Aunt Mary with a man or even heard her talk about anyone," Wynter said more to herself.

"Mmm, as far as I know there has been no one else. Timothy was it for her, and I am partially responsible for his death."

Wynter sat down across Anthony's lap and wrapped her arms around him in a supportive hug, in an attempt to offer what little comfort she could. "I'm sure if she'll give you a chance, she'll love you as much as I do."

A slow grin spread across Anthony's face. "Well, maybe not that much." He turned his face into Wynter's neck and kissed her.

Chapter Nine

Explorers, Noah thought harshly to himself. He got
so tired of explorers sometimes. Today was one of those
times. They didn't usually come in one man expeditions,
but this man did. He was determined too. Noah had
been blocking his path all day long. The guy was dressed
in layers at least as thick as himself. He waddled about
in the snow. It had to be hard to move around in all that
clothing, but he just wouldn't give up.

Noah hid behind a snow hill and raised his arm.
With a strenuous push of magic he forced an avalanche to
bar the human explorer's path. Noah's magic had grown
exponentially since the days when Ethan had spent
countless days teaching him and Wynter. What a laugh!
Wynter had no need of magic lessons. She was already

stronger than he or Ethan would ever be, but she played along.

All she wanted was to fit in. Noah could see that so easily; why couldn't Ethan see it? It seemed so obvious. Everything she had hid so carefully, she never complained. All she wanted was their acceptance and their love. She believed she'd had that too.

On the other side of the avalanche, Noah heard the man let out a frustrated growl. The sun was beginning to go down now. Surely, the man would return to his camp for the night. Determination, however, could border on dangerous at times.

The man pushed on looking for another way forward. That had been the third avalanche Noah had started today. He didn't know how many more he could start safely, and he was quickly running out of ideas to keep the human away.

What was wrong with this human? Didn't he understand that humans couldn't survive in this temperature? It used to be so easy to keep humans in the dark, but the more advanced the humans became, the more they wanted to know about the unknown. It was Noah's job to make sure that the South Pole people remained unknown to the humans.

Light flurries began to fall as the wind picked up. The weather could get harsh down here fast. If the man didn't turn back soon, Noah would be saving a human rather than hiding from one. Visibility was diminishing rapidly, and finally, the human explorer turned back. He had nearly waited too long. Worried, Noah followed the human, at a safe distance, back to his camp just to be sure that the human arrived safely.

It was late when Noah returned home. He was cold and tired. All he wanted was to help himself to a hot bowl of left over beef stew, thank you mom, and crawl into his warm bed.

The microwave beeped, and Noah removed the steaming bowl of beef stew. Before he could take a first bite there was a pounding on his door. What now? Noah wasn't in the mood for anything else tonight.

He opened the door, and Lorelei rushed in so quickly that she almost ran right into Noah. "Noah, it's horrible. Ethan is going to use Wynter to get in. It's so mean!"

"What? Lorelei, slow down. What are you talking about?"

"I heard some people in the shop today talking. I wanted to close and call you right away, but I knew you were working."

"It's better that you didn't. It would raise eyebrows, and you're our best source of information."

"Yeah. They know they can't get past the magical wards around the North Pole, alone. If Wynter Clause let's them in, though, no one can stop them, and there will be more of them than there are Clauses. There's a group of fifteen to twenty men ready to go. Ethan is going to appeal to Wynter saying he wants to talk to her. He'll tell her how he knows she didn't mean anyone any harm and how much he misses her. They said that he's even prepared to ask her for her help if it comes to that. They don't believe that she'll turn him down."

"She won't. She still loves him like a brother. She wants things to be okay between them badly enough to be blinded by her love for him."

"Once she lets him in, they all plan to go in together and overpower the Clauses. Do you think they stand a chance?"

"I think they stand a significant chance of getting in. As for overpowering them… that depends on how prepared the Clauses are. Wynter and Anthony will

neither one want to hurt the people who they lived along side, but protecting their daughter will have to come first I'm sure. Still, all Ethan has to do is catch them unaware and separated. His magic is no match for any of the Clauses'. Twenty on one, if it comes to that though, are some hard odds to overcome even with magic."

"What are we going to do?"

"How long do we have?"

"Less than two weeks. Is that long enough for another letter to get that far?"

"Maybe, maybe not. It wouldn't give them time enough to prepare for the attack... I'll call Kyson and Declan. I think it's time we took a trip to the North Pole."

"I'll start calling the others."

"Lorelei, you don't have to go."

"Of course I'm going. I believe in this thing."

How did he tell Lorelei he didn't want her to go without hurting her feelings? This wasn't going to be pretty. This wasn't something that was going to be settled with words. Noah was as sure of that as he was that Ethan could get to Wynter. The last thing he wanted was for

Lorelei to get involved in a war. He wanted to keep her as far away from the violence as he could.

"It's just that, who's going to run the shop while you're gone?"

"Once word gets around where I've gone and what we've done, there won't be any business to speak of anyway."

"That's my point, Lorelei. That shop is your livelihood... I can't ask you to give it up."

"You're not asking me to. I'm volunteering."

"You could be just as helpful here. You could be our lookout from here," Noah suggested.

"Noah! I chose my side already same as you. I don't see you trying to make any of the others stay behind," Lorelei pouted indignantly.

"Lorelei-"

"No, Noah. I'm going, and you can't stop me, so call the others."

"But-"

A bright red flush crept quickly up Lorelei's neck and face. Her eyes narrowed in warning. "I'm not discussing

this with you," she said and darted outside. The door slammed behind her with finality.

Noah closed his eyes and sighed in frustration. All he wanted was to protect Lorelei, but maybe he had gone about it the wrong way. No, he had obviously gone about it the wrong way. That much became apparent when she stormed off.

Someone would need to protect Anthony and Wynter's daughter once they got to the North Pole, yet it didn't make sense for it to be Anthony or Wynter. Wynter was way too strong to be put on the sidelines. Although Noah hadn't seen evidence of Anthony's new powers, he understood now that Anthony was a Clause he too had Clause magic. It, therefore, wouldn't make sense to sideline him either.

They would need someone gentle and kind, someone good with kids. They would need someone who could protect and care for the young girl. Lorelei would be ideal for the job. Fortunately that meant that Lorelei and the little girl would be hiding somewhere safe. It was the best Noah was going to get.

He walked back to the kitchen as he pulled his phone from his pocket. He looked longingly at his bowl of stew but started calling the others in instead.

Enoch was the first one to arrive. "What's up with Lorelei?" he asked.

"What do you mean?" Noah looked for clarification.

"She's outside stomping back and forth through the snow. She's actually worn a path down in your front yard. I know we're all upset about what's going on, but that seems a little extreme for Lorelei, don't you think?"

It did seem extreme for Lorelei. Maybe Noah's overprotective tendencies had enraged her more than he had imagined. Noah had believed she'd left. He hadn't thought for one second that Lorelei would still be out there in that cold. Could he go out there and get her to come inside, or would he only infuriate her more with his presence?

Before Noah could determine what to do Declan walked through the front door with Lorelei. Her face was stoic, frustration evident, and flushed. The rosy look was working for Lorelei, but Noah worried about what that rosy look had cost her. How cold had she allowed herself to get before finally coming back inside?

Noah moved his gaze up Lorelei's rosy cheeks to her striking blue eyes. Her eyes were as blue as the ocean hidden deep beneath the thick ice. She was staring back at Noah wide eyed with a storm raging in those familiar blue eyes. There was a challenge in her eyes meant for no one but Noah. He could see that much and knew that somehow he had alienated her himself. He couldn't say how things had gone so wrong. Was it truly unreasonable for him to want to protect her?

Lorelei broke eye contact first when she started quickly ripping her coat off as if she couldn't get out of it fast enough. Next to go were her gloves, scarf, and hat, and now Noah could see that the flush wasn't from the cold. She was sweating, over heated.

"You okay?" Enoch asked her.

Noah should have been the one to ask that. Lorelei's eyes slid back to Noah, and she answered, "I'm fine."

"Don't just stand there, man. Get the girl some water," Declan ordered Noah.

Noah moved robotically for the kitchen with Declan close on his heels. "What did you do?" Declan accused.

"Why do you automatically assume I did something?"

"Because Lorelei was pacing outside your house madder than I've ever seen her, and she doesn't want to talk about what's bothering her."

"And, that's my fault?"

Declan shrugged a negligent shoulder. "Tell me it isn't."

Noah sighed burdened heavily by the truth. "I tried to talk her in to staying here."

"Ohh, bad move, man."

"I just want her to stay safe."

"Would you ask me or Kyson to stay behind?"

"Of course not. You're guys."

"Word of advice, don't mention that in front of any of the girls. Would you ask Vivienne to stay behind?"

"No, she'd kick my butt."

"But, you did ask Lorelei to stay behind. Look at it from her point of view. It doesn't look like an attempt to keep her safe. It looks like you don't respect her as a viable part of this team."

"That's stupid. She's gathered more intel than anybody else. We wouldn't know as much as we do now without her. She's vital to this team."

"I know that, and you know that. But, does she?"

"She should."

"She needs to hear that."

"Where's that water?" Lorelei demanded as the kitchen door flew open. Noah knew she was mad, but it was hard to tell from her tone. Her voice was so kind, even when she was mad.

"Here you go," Declan offered tossing a bottle of water in Lorelei's direction.

"Hurry up. Everyone's here."

Declan and Noah followed Lorelei back to the living room where Kyson raised a suspicious eyebrow at Declan and Noah, but he was the only one to appear to notice that anything was amiss.

Noah looked at the six other people crowded into his small house. Vivienne looked ready to pounce. Most looked resigned, but Eddie looked like he was about to pee his pants. All eyes in the room focused on Noah waiting for instructions.

"Okay, you all know why we're here. We've been waiting on the team who intend to attack Santa Clause to make their move. Lorelei has more intel on the attack. Lorelei?"

"Twelve days from today a group plans to go to the North Pole fully aware that they can't get past the magical wards. They plan instead for Wynter Clause herself to get them inside."

Whispers of disbelief circled around the room. Noah wouldn't have believed it himself if he hadn't known his brother was just twisted enough to use someone he once called a friend.

"You all know Noah's brother. Ethan plans to appeal to Wynter convincing her he wants to talk. Then when she lowers the magical wards enough for Ethan to get through, the others plan to follow him through. They've got a team of at least fifteen, maybe more."

Enoch let out a low whistle. "That's some mighty odds."

"Do we know who the others are?" Kyson asked.

"No," Lorelei answered.

"And, there's too many it could be to narrow it down in the next twelve days," Eddie pointed out. "What can we do?"

"We go up there and ambush them before they can ambush the Clauses," Vivienne said with fire.

"Oh dear," Eddie mumbled. He started wringing his hands and fidgeting in his seat.

"Someone will need to stay behind to keep their ears open, Eddie, just to be sure that they don't call in more reinforcements," Lorelei said throwing a bone to Eddie who was clearly terrified. She looked to Noah with an expression that plainly dared him to contradict who should stay behind.

"I could do that!" Eddie offered excitedly. "I'm good at listening to others. I know everyone thinks I'm some paranoid conspiracy theorist, but I listen."

"No one thinks that, Eddie," Lorelei consoled. "We believe you. We're all on the same side here. I'm sure you would be perfect for the job, right everyone?"

Words of agreement and encouragement circled around the room probably more because they saw Eddie as a liability than as a decent spy.

"That's settled then," Noah announced taking back control of the meeting before Lorelei could pull anymore fast ones. "Eddie, do you have a way to get in touch with us if you hear anything important?"

"Oh." Eddie's face fell, and fear started overtaking him again.

"I have a set of sat phones. We can leave one with Eddie," Vivienne offered.

"Do I even want to know why you have a set of satellite phones?" Declan asked.

"They were a gift." Vivienne shrugged as if that were a perfectly normal gift that anyone might get.

"Good. The rest of us need to leave as soon as we can get everything together."

"It's a long trip between the South and North Poles unless you've got a sleigh and reindeer hidden somewhere," Kyson pointed out with a hint of teasing.

"The sooner the better, why don't we leave tomorrow morning?" Vivienne proposed.

"We all have jobs and other responsibilities to make arrangements for," Enoch reminded her.

"If you're too busy to get away, you can always stay here with Eddie."

"We're all busy," Noah interrupted, "but time is of the essence. How soon can everyone be ready?"

"I can be ready tomorrow morning. I'm just saying we're all busy," Enoch said.

"You're just trying to be contrary," Vivienne shot back.

"I can be ready in the morning," Kyson interrupted trying to diffuse the situation.

"Me too," Declan agreed.

"I'll be ready. Meet here?" Lorelei asked.

"Sounds good. I'm out of here. I've got arrangements to make," Vivienne dismissed.

"I better go too if I'm going to figure out something to do with the shop," Lorelei seconded.

"Actually, Lorelei, I can't do hair, nails, or any of that other girl beauty stuff, but I'm a real good businessman. If your other girls will stay on, I can keep the books and all for you while you're gone," Eddie offered.

"Really, Eddie? That would be great. I'll email you where everything is and passwords for everything."

"Sure, no problem. At least you're not leaving passwords with someone you're not sure you can trust."

"Is she sure she can trust you?" Enoch asked.

"You would trust him too. Quit giving Eddie a hard time," Lorelei defended.

It was true. Anyone in that room would have trusted Eddie. He was a paranoid little bugger, but he was trustworthy. He was right about being a good businessman too. If anyone could keep Lorelei's shop afloat while she was gone, it would be Eddie. The fact that Eddie was going to keep her business going made Noah feel fractional better.

"We'll meet back here at seven tomorrow morning," Noah announced.

Chapter Ten

Wynter sat on the couch at her parents' house clutching Noel to her chest. Noel was asleep completely oblivious to all the tension all around her. Anthony was pacing a hole in the floor... well, not literally, but he might as well have. All his pacing was only serving to ratchet Wynter's worry higher.

Mom was flitting around the room adjusting this and that as if Aunt Mary was overly critical about good housekeeping. Aunt Mary was anything but critical. She was so kind, loving, and full of fun energy. Wynter had never seen any side of Aunt Mary capable of making everyone so nervous.

Dad was sitting in his favorite recliner puffing on a pipe that Wynter had not seen him use since she was such a little girl. He was puffing so fast that she couldn't see the smoke leave his mouth but rather a small cloud of smoke hovering over his head.

"Dear, do you have to use that old pipe? The smell is horrid. Couldn't you put it away?" Mom asked.

Dad sat the pipe down on an end table. "Where is that girl?"

"I don't know," Mom answered.

"Maybe she heard I was going to be here and decided to boycott the family," Anthony suggested. Wynter couldn't tell if he was joking or not. If so, it wasn't a very funny joke.

Apparently Anthony didn't believe it was very funny either. Wynter hadn't thought it possible, but Anthony actually went a shade paler than he had been before. She knew that he was honestly scared of how Aunt Mary might react to his presence at the North Pole, or worse his marriage to Wynter, or worst of all, his plan to take over the job of Santa.

Surely Aunt Mary wouldn't do anything to harm him, but... then again, Wynter had never known anything about Timothy. That was before Wynter was born, but everyone who had been around back then were more nervous than she had ever seen them. Maybe there really was something to it. Wynter couldn't even imagine how she would react if someone ever hurt Anthony. Maybe there really was something to be nervous about.

"Anthony, maybe you should hold Noel. Aunt Mary will be less apt to attack if you're holding a baby, right?" Wynter suggested moving to where Anthony was pacing.

Anthony took Noel and kissed her sweet little head. She looked so much like Anthony. She had his hair and his eyes, and you couldn't see it now, but she had Anthony's amazing smile, except for those trademark dimples. Those dimples were all Santa.

"I'm here! What was so important?" Aunt Mary's voice rang through the house.

"Mary?" Santa called.

"Long time no see, big brother," Aunt Mary said with a wide, winning grin as she walked into the living room. Santa stood to greet her, but she altered course toward Wynter first. "There's my beautiful niece!"

She pulled Wynter into a super tight hug. Now that Wynter was paying attention, she wondered how she had never noticed before how strong Aunt Mary was.

"Where is that new husband and baby of yours?" Aunt Mary asked as she moved to find Anthony and

Noel. "YOU!" before anyone could react, Mary launched into action within less than a second she was standing in front of Anthony with a steak aimed at his heart while she struggled to take Noel from him.

Mom and Dad both pulled Mary back and pushed her across the room. All the while Wynter watched in astonishment as her favorite aunt attacked her husband and child.

"He's holding a baby. For Pete's sake, Mary, what were you going to do?" Mom admonished in her best mother tone.

"How did you get in here?" Mary hissed in Anthony's direction.

"Mary…"

"What are you doing here?" Mary asked as she advanced methodically. There was a crazed look in her eyes that Wynter had never imagined there before. It was a look that could only be described as murderous.

"Mary, I-I can explain," Anthony started.

"That better not be my great niece you're holding."

"Ah… Wynter? It might be best if you take Noel now."

"Aunt Mary? This is my husband, Anthony," Wynter introduced as if Mary wasn't standing there staring at Anthony like she wanted to kill him where he stood.

"Are you telling me that you married a blood sucking, demon following, monster and brought him to the North Pole?" She made it sound like a betrayal instead of love.

Wynter looked into eyes so similar to her own and wondered where all the violence she saw there could have possibly come from. "It's not like that."

"He's a vampire, Wynter, and what about you?" she asked turning on Santa. "Couldn't you protect your daughter?"

"Now, wait just a minute," Santa barked. "I take good care of my family."

"That's why you had to call in the rest of the family?"

"That is exactly why I called in the rest of the family. We have viable intel that the South Polers are planning an attack. I am fully aware that I am only one man, so I yes, I called for reinforcements."

As Santa argued with his baby sister, Wynter watched the pain flit across Anthony's face caused by Aunt Mary's statement. "Anthony is not a vampire!" Wynter shouted vehemently.

Aunt Mary whirled back to Wynter. "Don't tell me he's not a vampire. I've been hunting him for centuries. Did he tell you about the first time we laid eyes on one another?"

"Mary, we don't have to get into this right now, do we?" Anthony nearly begged.

She turned on him once again looking at him with lethal hatred burning hotly in her eyes. "How long ago was it, Anthony? Two-twenty? Two-thirty?"

"Two forty-three."

"Two hundred and forty-three years," Mary let out a low whistle. "That's a long time."

"I remember."

"So, do I, vampire."

"I told you he isn't a vampire. Not anymore," Wynter insisted.

Aunt Mary talked over Wynter as if she hadn't said anything at all. "I was young fresh to the hunt, my first week. The sun had barely begun to go down. I had not found anything any other night, and I didn't expect to find anything that night either. It's rare to find those suckers when you're still so new. What I found was the last thing I expected.

"I was walking down the sidewalk of a major road, not a back road or an ally way. All of the sudden I see this tall, lanky man stumbling down the sidewalk like he's drunk or something. My first thought was that this man was someone else's problem. The police could handle a drunk; I was looking for the monsters that the police couldn't handle. At least that's what I thought until I saw the blood. It was obvious then that he was more than just drunk, but I still didn't realize yet that he was a vampire. He wasn't acting like a typical vampire.

"Vampires are usually graceful and calculated in their movements. Anthony here was the least graceful person I think I had ever seen. As he got closer, I saw, despite dusk's waning light, that his face was covered in blood. There was blood dripping from his mouth.

"Then the craziest thing happens. This vampire ran right up to me and grabbed my arms not in attack but in desperation. Then, get this, he started asking me for help. He said he thought something was wrong."

"There was something wrong," Anthony deadpanned.

"Yeah, you were a blood sucking vampire who had just finished draining your victim."

"I hadn't," Anthony gritted out.

"Whatever," Aunt Mary cut him off, but Wynter wasn't going to have it.

"What had happened?" Wynter asked Anthony.

"I woke up choking on blood. I thought I was sick, but I didn't know how sick at the time. Later I would learn that this was typical for vampires who had just been turned. I couldn't remember anything that happened earlier that day, and I had never even imagined that vampires truly existed. I thought it was some horror story made up to get children to stay indoors after dark. It took me another two days to figure out what I had become."

"That's some sob story," Aunt Mary sneered.

"Aunt Mary?" This wasn't the Aunt Mary that Wynter had known all her life.

"I'm sorry, Wynter, but you can't show sensitivity to monsters who kill mercilessly."

"Anthony is not a merciless killer!" Wynter shrieked in anger at her aunt.

Noel stirred and started to cry in Anthony's arms. Aunt Mary was looking in shock at Wynter, who had never once raised her voice at her favorite aunt.

"Wynter, baby," Anthony said slowly, carefully, "maybe you should take Noel, reassure her that you're okay." It was a feeble distraction on Anthony's part. It wasn't working. Wynter moved right up into Mary's face. "Wynter, please don't say something you'll regret later."

"Me? Maybe someone should have told Aunt Mary that as she walked in the door, but it's too late for that now. Isn't it? Aunt Mary, you've got your facts all wrong. Anthony is not a killer."

"Honey," Mary cut her off, "I'll concede that maybe, just maybe, that at that first meeting maybe he had just turned and hadn't killed, yet, but he has killed."

Wynter opened her mouth and took a deep breath gearing up to let Mary have it. Anthony thought this might be a good time to set the record straight with Wynter. "Wynter, she's right. I have killed."

"I know that! We've talked about it before. How could I not know? What you don't know, Aunt Mary, is that he fought it with all he had every time, and afterwards no one hated him worse than he hated himself. He ran to the South Pole not to get away from you but to spare the world from himself. He loathed what he was. Did you know that he had written Daddy multiple letters asking him to help?"

"There's nothing even Santa can do to purge a vampire."

"You're right. Daddy didn't have the power to help him, but I did. Did you know that, Aunt Mary?"

"No, Wynter, listen to me, sweetheart. There's nothing you can do to change a vampire's predisposition."

"Uh, Mary..." Santa tried to stop her, but he was too late. What was said was said; there was no taking it back now.

"Wrong again," Wynter said with chilling calm. "My love for Anthony was strong enough. I was strong enough to make him a Clause, and that negated his vampire predisposition. When I tell you that he isn't a vampire anymore, I mean it, and he doesn't kill."

Mary stood motionless and just looked at Wynter like she couldn't believe what she had heard.

"I'd like to go home now," Wynter said approaching Anthony and a still sniffling Noel.

"Your father called Mary up here for a reason. We need her help. I'm not leaving until we've explained what's going on."

Wynter shook her head in defeat then reached for Noel. "You do what you feel like you have to do, but I can't stay here another minute."

Noel latched around Wynter's neck as soon as she was in Wynter's arms. Wynter hugged Noel close and went up on tip toe to kiss Anthony. Anthony kissed her goodbye, and she quickly turned for the door.

She looked back one last time to leave Mary with a parting warning. "If you hurt him, I will hunt you down the way you hunted him."

Chapter Eleven

Noah had been up most of the night. He had to make work arrangements. Someone would need to keep an eye on the explorer who had been trying so hard to get through, and he was probably with an entire team somewhere. Besides the explorer, all the animals on Noah's case load would need tending.

He decided that it would be best not to tell anyone outside of work he was leaving. News would get around soon enough, and Ethan would no doubt be warned. That didn't mean that Noah had to hurry the process along though. He knew that if he told his parents, that Ethan would know before Noah even left. Who knew, maybe his father was a part of the group going up to attack the Clauses.

He had finally gotten a couple hours sleep only because he knew he needed some kind of rest, but that had been all he could afford himself before getting back up to pack. It was almost six now, and he was finishing up.

"You should really lock your doors," Declan's voice carried through the house.

"Hey, you're up early."

"Couldn't sleep, too much adrenalin. I figured it wouldn't be long before Kyson showed up." Kyson was a notorious morning person. He had most likely been up as long as Noah. "How you hanging in there?"

"I'm trying not to think about it too much," Noah answered honestly. "Once upon a time, my biggest worry was that Ethan and Wynter were in league together to sabotage a snowball fight... It's a far cry from worrying they'll destroy each other."

"That it is... It makes the rest of us look more like crybabies. We're worried about our businesses, what our families will think, or how things will be different when we get back, but for you, whether you get involved or not, you have to watch family pitted against family. That's what I think people like Owen don't get. As much as they claim not to hold the same prejudices as their family, they still see Wynter as a Clause. To them she's an outsider. She's different, not like us. They can't see her as family to you."

Noah stared at Declan dumbfounded. "When did you get so sensitive?"

"Yeah, yeah, just keep it to yourself. I have a reputation to maintain."

"What reputation is that?"

"I am a certifiable hot head, and a jack of all sports." Declan was an instructor teaching anything from sledding to hockey. Sledding didn't really demand as much instruction; therefore, usually only women attempting to flirt took his classes on sledding. His hockey classes consisted of mostly young kids in the beginning stages of the game. Declan's other specialties were in snowboarding and skiing, but he would take on any challenge customers presented.

"For some reason that worries me. You exercise for a living, making you stronger than most, and you have a short fuse."

"And, that is why people don't cross me."

"If only they knew how level headed you really are," Noah teased.

"We all have to have our own trick. Your job alone keeps people in line."

"My job?"

"Yeah, that's right. You're a bad to the bone ranger. No one in their right mind messes with a ranger."

"So, what does that make Ethan and his band of merry men?"

"Out of their right mind."

Declan and Noah were still laughing their heads off when Kyson got there. "What's so funny?" he asked.

"We were just talking about job perks. Did you get everything squared away?" Declan asked.

"Yeah, no problem." Kyson was a statistician. Neither Noah nor Declan pretended to see the appeal, but Kyson enjoyed it. He claimed that it was calming, predictable, and just his speed. The numbers and data kept him busy without overwhelming or stressing him. It made it easier for him to keep his work life and personal life separate. "You got anything to eat around here?" he asked opening doors and going through cabinets.

"Help yourself. There's some eggs and bacon in the fridge that will probably be bad by the time we get back," Noah offered.

"How long do you think this will take?"

"No way to tell. The travel itself will take a while."

"Yeah."

"Knock, knock," Enoch called from the front door.

"Good timing," Declan answered. "You just won stove duty."

"Come again?"

"Eggs and bacon, they won't be any good when we get back. We were just making plans to cook what was left. Thought it would be best if the next person through the door received the honor of cooking. Isn't that right, Kyson?"

"That's right."

"How diplomatic."

"How did you take care of work stuff?" Kyson wondered.

Enoch was a lawyer and a good one. That may have been another reason why he played devil's advocate so much. Everyone knew that if Enoch was your lawyer, your case was as good as won.

"I passed my cases to someone else. I had to call all my clients last night. Not all of my clients were real happy, but the guy I handed my case load to was thrilled."

"You gave all your cases to one person?" Kyson asked curiously.

"Yeah, isn't that a little too much for one person?" Noah seconded.

"Nah, he's the new guy, doesn't get much work, but he's good."

"Let's get this party started!" Vivienne yelled from the front door.

"Come on in. We're just waiting on Lorelei," Noah answered.

"I'm here," came Lorelei's voice from behind Vivienne.

"Okay, we know how Lorelei took care of work. What about you Vivienne?" Enoch asked.

"Seven on, seven off. I'm off right now. If we're not back in a week, I'll deal with it then."

Vivienne was a nurse in the ER. The adrenaline rush Noah got, but he had a hard time picturing Vivienne as the warm and fuzzy caregiver. Luckily he had never been treated in the ER, which was an odd stat in his line of work.

"Breakfast is served," Enoch announced sliding a plate of bacon and a platter of eggs onto the table.

"I didn't know you were so domestic," Vivienne teased.

"Well, a man has to learn to survive when he's on his own."

"Looks like everyone is early. Eat up. We still leave at seven prompt," Noah said before walking out of the kitchen to start loading bags. It didn't get past him that Lorelei hadn't said more than two words. Maybe she wasn't much of a morning person, or maybe she was still mad.

Noah had been working for fifteen minutes to get everyone's luggage into two cars, when Declan and Kyson came out. "Let us finish up. Go inside and eat," Kyson told him.

The other three were talking when Noah came in and took a seat. "Do you think Rudolph is real?" Enoch asked.

"No," Noah responded.

"You sure?"

"Yep."

"Too bad that would have been something to see," Vivienne smiled.

Lorelei got up and went to the sink without a word. She started rinsing dishes and loading the dishwasher. She would rather clean his house than carry on a conversation with him. Okay, she was definitely still mad.

They hit the road by seven and were on their way to the nearest helicopter, which was still a day's travel away. A day to the helicopter, another day to the tip of Africa, and then another week up to Greenland. From there they would take another helicopter ride to the Arctic.

"Has anybody thought about the travel time?" Vivienne asked once the helicopter was up in the air.

Noah nodded, but didn't say a word. He was curious if anyone else had given any real thought to the travel time.

"It will give us time to think," Enoch approached.

"Or, time to be at each other's throats," Vivienne countered.

"We'll be in very close proximity for roughly the next week and a half," Declan stated.

"I think the hard part won't be the close proximity. The hard part will be when we get to the Arctic. Can we find the North Pole without tearing each other apart?" Kyson asked.

"It's a little late to ask ourselves that," Noah pointed out. "Either we can work together as a team, or we will be of no help to the Clauses."

The others looked around the group, but Noah had his sights on Lorelei. He was acutely aware that she still had not spoken to him, and he wondered how much longer he could stand her silence.

Chapter Twelve

"Mary, you shouldn't have done that," Santa scolded.

"What should I do? Allow the vampire to continue hurting my niece?" Mary shot back.

"I would never hurt Wynter," Anthony stated as calmly as he could, "but I do believe that this group we've been warned about might hurt her and Noel." Anthony fought back his instincts to lash out at Mary for implying that he was hurting Wynter.

"First South Polers and now vampires," Mary sighed. "What kind of operation are you running up here, brother dear?"

"Mary, I know you and I don't have a pleasant past together, but we both love Wynter and Noel. Neither of us wants to see them hurt. Can't we, please, put our own past behind us just this once?"

"Are you suggesting that we work together?"

"Yes." Mary didn't like that idea at all. Anthony knew that she wouldn't, but the evidence was clear in both her tone and her body language.

"Well, I'm suggesting that we all work together and fight less," Santa said. "Anthony isn't the same person you met all those years ago. You may have met him on his first night as a vampire, but I met him on his last. Wynter did change him, and he's changed her. They've changed each other, and there's one thing I'm sure of. She loves him very much, and if you insist on alienating him, you will alienate her... While you think about that, have a seat so that we can bring you up to date."

"I have a better idea. Let's get Mary something to eat. Give her a few minutes to settle, and you can tell everyone at once when they all get here," Mrs. Clause suggested.

Anthony nodded his agreement. Santa puffed out his frustration and led the way to the kitchen.

"Cookies?" Mrs. Clause offered to Anthony.

"Thank you, Mrs. Clause." Anthony sat down at the island with a large plate of sugar cookies.

"Ugh, I don't know how you can even look at another cookie after Christmas Eve," Santa groaned.

"I love cookies."

"And, I love that you love them," said Mrs. Clause. "It's nice to have someone around here who appreciates my cookies."

"He's got you all under his spell," Mary groaned.

"Now, you know that's not possible," Santa refuted.

"Actually it is," Anthony said between bites. He immediately regretted it when he realized that all eyes in the room were trained on him.

"What makes you say that?" Santa asked.

"We, uh… we tried it once. It was when Noah was still fairly young and immensely curious. He wanted to know how my, uh… magic worked. He sort of volunteered Wynter. We tried to tell her she didn't have to, but you know Wynter. I wasn't sure that it would work; in fact, I thought more like you, that it wouldn't work at all. Turned out she was susceptible though. She was very responsive, yet…"

"Yet what?" Santa pushed.

"She remembered the whole thing. Well, I don't remember anything from when I was on the other side of things. It was curious."

"You admit you put her under your spell?" Mary asked cautiously.

"Well, yes, but it was only for a few minutes."

"She's still under your spell just like my brother and his wife are now."

"No, that's not true. I never even tried it on men. As far as I know, it wouldn't have worked on Santa at all. Besides, I don't do that anymore."

"But, you could?"

"I don't know. That's not who I am anymore. I guess I could do it just as easily as you can."

"Show her what your magic can do," Mrs. Clause suggested. She was one of Anthony's biggest supporters. She told him all the time how strong his magic was and swore that it was stronger than any other she had seen who had married into the family.

"All right." He couldn't let down Mrs. Clause. Anthony got up and walked back into the living room trusting that the others would follow. He looked at the roaring fire burning bright in the fireplace and doused it

with a shower of snow flurries. Anthony smiled as smoke spiraled up the chimney. "Wynter taught me that one my first week."

"I didn't like it anymore when she did it either. Replace the fire if you will," Santa instructed.

Anthony replaced the fire as he had been told, and Mrs. Clause smiled excitedly at Mary. "You see Mary? Clause magic, much more powerful than anything a vampire has ever possessed. Now everyone come back to the kitchen. I've made a big pot of chicken and rice. Anthony, why don't you call Wynter and see if you can get her back up here before the rest of her aunts and uncles get here?"

"I can try, but Wynter was pretty fired up. I don't think she's too happy with me right now either."

"Good, maybe she's starting to see the light," Mary spouted off.

"Mary, I'm sorry to say it, but I don't think you're stubborn streak is helping the situation," Mrs. Clause said.

"My stubborn streak?" Mary admonished.

"Yes, that's right. It's a Clause trait that you, Santa, and Wynter all have in common."

Mary looked Anthony from head to toe and back again. "I don't trust him," she said.

"No one is asking you to trust him, only to give him a chance… for Wynter's sake."

"Knock, knock, anybody home?" a deep male voice boomed through the house.

"Israel!" Mary squealed like a little girl and ran out of the kitchen.

Anthony had never seen Mary Clause so joyful before. It was like she flipped a switch and became a person he didn't know. When Mary returned, she was being carried by a giant of a man with one arm around her waist. The man was tall and broad, built like a solid wall of muscle, but it was his playful eyes that told the most about the man. Anthony had met Israel only once at his and Wynter's wedding, but he had learned that Israel was a big, fun loving teddy bear.

"How's it going, Anthony? I can't wait to see my great niece. Where is she?" Israel asked as he put Mary's feet back on the floor.

"She's with Wynter, at home."

"So, what were we all called up here for if it's not to meet Noel?"

"You thought meeting my first grandchild was the big emergency?" Santa questioned.

"I hoped. Didn't bring the family just in case."

"That probably wasn't a bad idea. Maybe when it comes time you can suggest a good place to hide Noel," Anthony said.

"Okay, what is going on here?" Israel asked all business.

"Oh no," Mrs. Clause interrupted. "We're waiting until everyone gets here. Anthony, I believe you were about to call Wynter up here for some chicken and rice soup."

"Yes, ma'am," Anthony responded and torpedoed to the phone while everyone else got bowls and spoons.

"Wynter, your mom really wants you to come back up for lunch. She made chicken and rice soup."

"Is Aunt Mary still there?"

"Yes, you know we need her here."

"Then I'm staying here with Noel. Did she at least agree to stay and help?"

"Actually, we haven't talked to her about any of it yet."

"What are you all doing up there? Catching up on old times?" Wynter snapped.

"Wynter, please don't be angry. We need their help. Your mom wants to wait and tell everyone at once. Israel is here. Are you coming up?"

"No."

"Do you want me to bring you and Noel a bowl of soup?"

"I'm perfectly capable of feeding us."

"I know you are, baby. The soup is already done; you wouldn't have to bother cooking."

"You say that like it's some great hardship to cook. You could come down here and eat with me and Noel."

"Wynter, please don't do this. Please. I don't want to come between you and your family."

"Anthony, I'm not willing to sacrifice you to keep my family."

"Wynter, no one is asking you to... Mary," Anthony called.

"Still here, blood sucker," she replied.

"Does Wynter have to sacrifice me to keep you in her life?"

"What's he talking about, Mar?" Israel's deep voice asked.

"Anthony Phillips is a vampire."

"Was a vampire. He hasn't made any secret of that. No one is more thrilled than him that Wynter was able to reverse that. He was positively gitty about the subject when it came up at the wedding reception."

"He's gotten to you too," Mary spit.

"Mary, listen to yourself. Is this about protecting Wynter or is it a personal vendetta?" Israel accused.

Anthony tuned them out with a force of will. "I really think you should get up here," he whispered into the phone.

"And, I really think you should get down here," Wynter sobbed. Yep, that did it. Wynter was crying.

"I'm coming, baby. Just hold on." Anthony dropped the phone back to the end table and called over his shoulder. "Santa, Mrs. Clause, I've got to go."

Mrs. Clause was there before Anthony could make it out the door. She laid a gentle hand on his shoulder. "Let me go."

"But-"

"I know. Let me go. If it doesn't work I'll give you a call."

"Okay," Anthony nodded.

Chapter Thirteen

Noah was so tired of getting off one aircraft only to hop onto another. They'd been gone for a week now, and their absence must have been noticed by now. He wondered what everyone was saying and where their families thought they had gone. He was sure his family suspected that he had hot footed it up to the North Pole. It wouldn't take long before they put two and two together and told the others' families where they had gone as well.

Would anyone come after them only to get caught in the middle of a war zone? How far behind them would Ethan and the others be? With better connections and more time to plan, there was an off chance that the others could catch up to them before they made it to the North Pole... especially if Noah's family figured out where he had gone? All Noah knew for sure right about now was that they were wasting time they didn't have.

"I'm driving," Vivienne announced.

"There's only three," Declan responded.

The rental place only had three snow mobiles left, and that was the only way to get any further north without a team of sled dogs or reindeer.

"Yeah, and I'm going to be driving one," Vivienne insisted.

"I'm not riding with you or anyone else for that matter. I drive," Declan pushed back.

Vivienne shot a look at Declan that could burn though his skull had she been a Clause.

"I don't mind riding behind you," Kyson offered Vivienne.

Noah rolled his eyes. He just bet that Kyson didn't mind, more like a dream come true.

"I'll ride with Declan," Lorelei quickly put in.

"I guess that just leaves you and me," Enoch said to Noah. "Just make sure you keep your hands to yourself."

"So, it's settled then?" Noah double checked.

"Why don't us girls stick together?" Vivienne wanted to know.

A slow devious smile spread across Declan's face before he said, "Because not all of us are fond of snuggling up with other guys."

"Uggh, who said we wanted to snuggle up with you either?" Vivienne returned.

"It's okay. I don't mind," Lorelei smoothed over. "Come on, Declan. Let's go." She tugged on his arm to get him moving toward the snow mobile.

It was a rather bold move for someone as shy as Lorelei and a lot more attention than she had paid Noah since the morning they left the South Pole. She had not said a word to him the whole trip. Noah would have given almost anything to have her ride with him, but it just wasn't meant to be.

"Fine, let's go," Vivienne huffed in Kyson's direction. He wasted no time scooting up behind her and wrapping his arms around her waist.

A glance back in Lorelei's direction showed her arms wrapped tightly around Declan's waist. Noah bit back a snide remark recognizing it as the jealousy it was. Declan didn't have feelings for Lorelei; in addition, he knew that Noah did have feelings for Lorelei. Declan was one of his very best friends. Noah trusted him, but still, that didn't make Lorelei's arms around Declan any easier to ignore.

"You coming?" Enoch called over his shoulder.

"Yeah."

It was a long way left to go through the snow and ice, the harsh weather of the North Pole. Lucky for them they were used to the harsher weather where humans didn't dare linger. It didn't mean, however that they didn't feel the cold. No one knew how to find the North Pole, no one except a Clause that is. Well, Anthony had managed to find it somehow, but he had been desperate to find the woman that he loved. Noah seriously doubted that anyone from the South Pole was going to just stumble upon Santa's workshop.

It was a big enough place. The land they occupied was vast. It had to be with two houses, a toy workshop, and reindeer stables. Noah had been taken aback when he visited over a year ago at just how big it was. It must take some serious magic to conceal any place that large, but if anyone could wield that much magic, it would be the Clauses.

Noah did his best to guide Everett, but disappointingly he was just as lost as the others. When he had been to visit Wynter he had flown in a magic sleigh with Santa himself. The whole situation itself had been such a novelty that he had hardly paid attention to how they got there. He was sure, however, if he had paid better attention, it still wouldn't have done him any good. Things looked so different from on the ground than they had flying above it.

They had been riding for hours when Vivienne pulled ahead of the pack and came to a stop. She got off and began stomping around in the deep snow. Her boots sunk out of sight with every step she took. Kyson stood back and watched her with a cool indifference as he leaned up against the snow mobile.

"This is ridiculous!" Vivienne started as the other engines cut off. "It is freezing out here. How long can we continue to ride around in circles? I don't like wondering aimlessly in a frozen tundra, Noah."

"I know, but do you have any better idea how to find a place fortified with magic to keep people like us out."

"I thought their point was to keep the humans out."

"If I were a Clause, I would be just as worried about some random hater from the South Pole determined to kill me, more so," Enoch pointed out.

"Yeah? Well, I'm too cold to keep driving around aimlessly," Vivienne complained.

"Like I said if you have any better ideas, I'm all ears," Noah agreed.

"We're all cold," Declan stepped in. "That doesn't change anything."

"We could trade places," Kyson added in a nonchalant tone.

"Oh, you'd like that wouldn't you, driving yourself," Vivienne shot back.

Kyson gave a slight grin and said, "Actually, I was rather enjoying the view from where I was, but if you're really that cold you could hide from the wind behind me."

Vivienne looked at Kyson with so much contempt that Noah was sure she was about to attack.

"It's true. I've been ducked down behind Declan to hide from the wind, and it really does help," Lorelei added tentatively.

Vivienne looked at Lorelei with betrayal shinning in her eyes, causing Noah to take an instinctive step between the two women.

"You're lucky you have a girl fighting your battles for you," Vivienne told Kyson then gestured for him to take the driver's position.

Kyson chuckled, and Vivienne glared as she climbed on behind him. "Better hold on tight, Viv."

Noah had never heard anyone ever call Vivienne anything other than Vivienne, and as a reward she wrapped her arms around Kyson's middle so tightly that it knocked the wind out of him.

Noah started up the engine, and they once again started their long pointless search.

Chapter Fourteen

"Wynter," Mom called from the door.

"Mom? What are you doing here, and where is Anthony?"

"I told him to let me come instead. Where's Noel?" she asked as she rounded the corner into the living room.

"She's in the yard with Roscoe. She started screaming for him the second she spotted him. He won't let anything happen to her," Wynter tried to reassure her mom.

"Oh, I'm sure he won't, but what do you think Noel would possibly need protecting from here?"

"Oh, I don't know, Aunt Mary."

"That isn't fair."

"Isn't it?"

"Mary would never hurt Noel… she wouldn't purposely hurt you either." Mom sat down on the couch next to Wynter, close but still giving her space.

"I used to believe that."

"You still believe that," Mom informed. "What she said did hurt you, though, whether she meant for it to or not. That's hard to process that your favorite aunt could possibly hurt you, but she did."

"She was so mean to him."

"Yes. She was. That was unfortunate."

"Unfortunate? It was more than unfortunate."

"Wynter, I know you're hurting right now, but try to put yourself in Mary's shoes. Could you ever forgive someone who played a part in Anthony's death?"

"Absolutely not, but he didn't have anything to do with the murder. She won't listen long enough for him to tell her that."

"Would you?"

"Would I what? Listen?"

"Yes. If you found Anthony lying dead in a pool of blood with some unknown vampire sitting over him drinking him dry, the vampire's face covered in blood, would you have stopped to listen to what the vampire had to say?"

"He wasn't an unknown vampire. Aunt Mary had met him before. He asked for her help that first night. Had she just tried to help him that night he wouldn't have been anywhere near Aunt Mary's fiancé."

"Wynter, can you hear yourself?"

"Yes, she didn't even try."

"Think about what you're saying for a minute. How could Aunt Mary have helped Anthony when your father could not?"

"I don't know, but she could have done something," Wynter argued desperately.

"Had she been able to help Anthony more than two hundred years ago, he never would have been in the South Pole in order to meet you."

Wynter paused to watch her mom's calm face. She was serious, and she was right. If there had been any way to reverse what had been done to Anthony that night, if he could once again have been mortal, he wouldn't have ever set foot in the South Pole. He couldn't have survived living there even if he had gotten past the rangers, but more importantly Anthony would have died long before Wynter had even been born.

"What could she have done to help him?" Mom asked.

What indeed? Was there a way to reverse the damage done by being turned? If so, Anthony never found it after two centuries of searching. There was no other way.

"How does it feel?"

"How does what feel?" Wynter questioned.

"The damage for Anthony had already been done by the time he sought help. You know as well, or better, than any of us that there was only one way to undo what had been done. In order to help him, Mary would have had to used the same once in a lifetime magic that you used. That would have made Anthony your uncle... How does that feel?"

"What do you mean how does that feel? How do you think it feels? It feels disgusting. It feels depressing. It feels like a betrayal on both their parts." Wynter was mad. She was mad that her own mother would even suggest such a thing. She was mad that Aunt Mary was ever given the chance to love Anthony the way she did.

Without permission tears started flowing freely down Wynter's cheeks… again.

"You see? Anthony and Mary were never meant to be friends. Things worked out just the way they were supposed to. God had a plan for Anthony's life, and that plan was to end up here, with you."

Wynter did a face plant into her mom's shoulder and cried harder. "She hates him."

"It's okay," Mom cooed in Wynter's ear as she rubbed soothing circles on her back.

"How will it ever be okay?" Wynter asked begging for an answer.

"I don't know yet, baby girl, but we won't give up. I don't want you to give up either, and everything will work out. You didn't give up on finding a cure for Anthony."

"I'd never give up on Anthony," Wynter said a little too vehemently.

"Exactly, don't give up on him now. He'll win over Mary just like he won over the rest of us."

"How? You agree with Aunt Mary."

"No, now, that's not what I said. I can understand where Mary is coming from that doesn't mean that I agree. I just think we should give them some time to work through this on their own."

"That doesn't make it any easier to know that my favorite aunt hates my husband."

"No, I imagine it doesn't... Do you know what I don't imagine is any easier?"

"What?"

"Being stuck in the middle. Anthony was torn between staying to do what he thought was right for his young family and following you out in a show of solidarity. Then after calling you, he felt the need to come running to check on you."

"Why didn't he?"

"I told you, because I said so."

"That is such a mother answer," Wynter laughed.

"It is, isn't it? Doesn't make it any less true, and I thought this time it would be best to have your mother. Anthony is too personally involved on a couple levels. I'm a little more objective. All he wants is to make you happy."

"And, you don't?"

"Of course I want to see you happy, but I've learned that in life sometimes you have to endure moments of strife and even pain to get to long term happiness. I could have your father send Mary away, but eventually it would eat you up inside."

Wynter was saved from thinking too long on that statement by a loud huffing at the back door. She stood and went to the back door to meet Roscoe and Noel. "Milk!" Noel cried loudly.

After fixing a sippy cup of milk, Wynter laid down on the couch with a very sleepy Noel. Noel's nap had been interrupted, and she was feeling the effects of it now.

"Are you okay?" Mom asked.

"As okay as I'm going to be," Wynter answered.

"I'm going to head back to the house. Will you be okay?"

"I'm fine."

"All right, Israel is here. Come up as soon as you can. Can I tell Anthony you're okay?"

"Yes, tell him that Noel and I are just taking a nap."

"I will, and Wynter... I want you to think about what I said."

"Yes, ma'am."

Chapter Fifteen

"Should I go check on her?" Anthony worried.

"Have some patience, son. Her mother raised her for twenty-one years," Santa advised.

"Yeah, until she ran away at twenty-one," Anthony smarted back. "I mean… I'm so sorry, Santa. I shouldn't have said that."

"No, no, it's true. She did do that. Just wait it out though."

"Eat your soup, Anthony. If there's one thing I've learned over the years, sometimes it is best not to get involved," Israel shared his wisdom.

"That's right. Enjoy your lunch while you can," Santa laughed.

"Where are the other three anyway?" Israel asked.

"On their way I assume."

"It's not like North to be late for anything."

"He had a pressing engagement."

"Say what you mean," Mary told her brother. "He was hunting," she said glaring in Anthony's direction.

"Mary," Santa said warningly.

"It's fine. She's correct," Anthony said.

"Any friends of yours?" Mary taunted.

"Hardly, none of my friends are vampires. Most of my friends are in fact here at the North Pole."

"Most of?"

"Yes, most of."

"Where would the others be right now?"

"If I had to venture a guess, I'd say the South Pole."

Mary stared at Anthony for a moment before spitting in a disgusted voice, "A vampire with ties to the South Pole."

"That's enough, Mary," Israel said authoritatively. "You would know that the ties Anthony has to the South Pole are the same that Wynter has if you had bothered to come to the wedding."

Tears filled Mary's eyes. "You think I didn't want to be here for my own niece's wedding? I wanted to be here! Maybe I could have talked her out of marrying this blood craving monster."

Anthony leaped from his chair causing his bowl of soup to splatter in several directions. "That is too much!"

He could feel all the blood rushing to his face and his blood pressure rising, and it had nothing to do with Mary referring to him as a blood craving monster. He knew enough to know that had been true, but he had never been more scared of anything as he had while he and Wynter were engaged. He had lived every minute in fear that Wynter would come to her senses and choose not to marry him after all.

"You have no right to come up here and try to tear my family apart!" Anthony was screaming now. He couldn't stop himself. Mary had finally hit on Anthony's biggest fear.

"Whoa, hey! Settle down. Back off my baby sister man," said a new comer. He was shorter than Israel and much, much thinner. He was a relatively little man, but he was deceptively strong. Joseph was the last in line before Mary.

Anthony had laughed at the wedding at stories about all the things Joseph had done as a child to terrorized his baby sister, but Santa had assured Anthony that Mary and Joseph had been inseparable as children. Anthony had been amused by the idea that the two closest of the siblings had so aptly been named Mary and Joseph. It was a match made in heaven if Anthony had ever seen one. No one else said anything, and Anthony thought it best to keep that little tidbit to himself.

"I can handle him," Mary boasted.

"In that case, you back off my nephew," Joseph changed his mind.

"Leave it to Joseph to walk in and immediately try to stir the pot," Israel said thumping Joseph on the back and pulling him in for a hug.

Joseph moved around the table hugging everyone before he stopped and looked around nervously. "Where's Wynter and her mom? Is there something wrong with Wynter?"

"No, nothing like that," Santa assured his brother.

"It seems Mary has been verbally attacking Anthony, and Wynter got mad and left," Israel summarized.

"Ah, is it the vampire thing?" Joseph asked.

"Thank you, someone who agrees with me,"
Mary sighed.

"I didn't say I agreed with you. It did sort of throw
me for a loop at first, but really Anthony doesn't act
anything like any vampires I've run across."

"Take my word for it. He was."

"Meh," Joseph shrugged. "So where's my
great niece?"

"She's with Wynter," Anthony puffed still trying to
calm himself down. "I think I should go check on her."

Anthony moved to the back door and reached for the
handle just as it swung open. Mrs. Clause walked in...
without Wynter. "Oh, excuse me, Anthony."

"Where's Wynter?"

"She said to tell you she was fine. She and Noel are
going to take a nap."

"Oh... maybe I'll just go down there and check on
them myself."

"She's fine, Anthony. Come eat," Mrs. Clause
insisted. She looped her arm around Anthony's and
tugged him back to the table.

Anthony sat down, and Santa threw a towel in Anthony's direction. He cleaned up the spilled soup that made a mess when he stood suddenly before at Mary's remark. Mrs. Clause poured herself and Joseph each a bowl of soup.

"How are you, Joseph?" Mrs. Clause greeted.

"Can't complain. So, what's up?"

"We're still waiting on North," Mary provided bitingly.

"Oh, hey, that's right. Where is the responsible one?"

"Working."

"When can we expect him?"

"He said tonight by the latest," Santa supplied.

"So, soon then," Joseph translated. "What about Star?"

The four siblings looked around the room at each other then in unison said, "Fashionably late."

Anthony didn't know Star well enough to get that impression, but he didn't doubt her own brothers and sisters knew her well enough. The fashionable part he could see however. He remembered Star from the wedding in her red knee length dress. It was gathered a lot and had a lot of material with thin straps. It even had rhinestones on one side where it gathered underneath her bust line. She had paired it with rhinestone jewelry that Anthony barely recalled and sky high black heels with red underbelly that Anthony distinctly remembered click clacking across the floor. Mostly Anthony only remembered the outfit at all, because he remembered Wynter bragging on how beautiful her Aunt Star looked.

They ate their soup with relatively friendly chatter, not that Anthony or Mary joined in. Mary kept a close eye on Anthony, and Anthony kept a close eye on the door. Wynter still hadn't come back up.

"Anthony, dear, why don't you take them a bowl of soup? You're not going to relax until you talk to her yourself, and Star isn't known for her timeliness," Mrs. Clause advised.

Anthony nodded despondently and stood to fix soup for Wynter and Noel.

"I'll go with him," Mary announced pushing to her feet.

"Mary, sit down," Santa said gruffly. Mary must have understood that it wasn't a suggestion, because she dropped back into her chair with a growl.

"Look who I found out stomping around in the snow!" came a higher pitched voice very similar to Santa's. Star. "Have you all seen that big bear they have? Noel was riding piggy back while the huge beast stomped behind Wynter."

Anthony dumped the ladle back into the pot of soup and spun around. "Wynter?" He rushed into the foyer and swooped Wynter up into his arms. Noel was already in Star's arms, who squeezed past Anthony and Wynter.

"Isn't this the cutest baby you've ever seen?" Star cooed as she walked into the kitchen with the others.

"Are you okay?" Anthony asked Wynter quietly, drown out by the others gushing over Noel.

Wynter nodded her head silently and buried her face in Anthony's shoulder. It wasn't as affirmative as he had hoped for, but he would take what he could get.

"Wynter, get in here and eat," Santa ordered in a gentle voice that gave way the fact that he now held Noel.

Wynter sighed and marched into the kitchen to face her aunt.

Chapter Sixteen

Noah slowed to a stop then killed the engine. This was getting ridiculous. They were never going to find the North Pole this way.

"What do you want to do?" Declan asked. He, too, must have realized how fruitless this search would be.

Noah pushed off the snow mobile and stretched his sore legs. Legs, arms, back, he was sore from head to toe. They had been riding for hours and hours, and it was getting them nowhere. Still unsure what to do, Noah lifted his painfully frozen hands to his face and cupped them around his mouth. "Santa!"

"What's he doing?" Vivienne asked.

"Maybe his brain froze over," Declan teased.

Kyson sighed. "You don't seriously think that he can hear you, do you? Even if he could, why would he answer a group of South Polers?"

"He knows me. If he can hear, he'll answer."

"You don't know he can hear you," Enoch pointed out.

Noah ignored the nay saying and raised his hands to his mouth again, but this time Lorelei's voice joined his, "Santa!"

"Ughh," Declan grumped before cupping his hands too around his mouth. "Santa!"

"I can't believe this is our best shot. Well, what are we waiting for?" Kyson asked the others, and they all cupped their hands around their mouth and screamed out into the frozen tundra, "SANTA!"

❄ ❄ ❄

"Did anyone hear that?" Santa asked.

"Hear what?" Star asked smiling as bright as a star.

"I don't know. It sounded like… It is. It's my name… Everyone just be quiet a minute."

Everyone in the room, with the exception of Noel, froze. The sound of Noel playing with her spoon and near empty bowl was the only sound. Wynter didn't hear anything; she especially didn't hear anyone calling her father's name. She closed her eyes as she strained to hear. Then it happened. She heard it. It wasn't just one voice but several muffled voices calling out Santa's name. One unmistakable voice stood out, Noah.

"It's Noah! I hear him!" Wynter cried. With a wave of her hand, she amplified the sound so that everyone could hear.

"SANTA!"

"Where are they?" Anthony asked.

"Who are they?" Israel asked.

"Noah is our friend from the South Pole," Wynter explained.

"Very polite young man," Santa tacked on.

"That's all well and good, kid, but that is more than one person," Joseph pointed out. "Who are the others?"

"Friends of his maybe. Noah wouldn't lead an ambush up here. He was the one who warned us there was trouble brewing in the first place," Anthony said.

"Everyone stay here. I'm going to get them," Santa instructed.

"I don't like it," Mary said, but Santa paid her no attention. He was already gone, leaving nothing in his wake but a dying build up of magic.

"I've never seen anyone from the South Pole before. This should be fun," Star smiled.

"Yeah, fun," Israel mumbled more so to himself.

"Brace yourselves," Wynter said as soon as she felt the intense magic filling the room again.

Santa appeared again in the kitchen, but this time he had six others with him. They all held hands in a tight circle around the table.

"Noah!" Wynter squealed. She moved to Noah and pulled him out of the circle into a hug.

"You're so warm," Noah chattered.

"How long were you wondering around looking for this place?" Anthony asked seriously.

"We've been searching for hours," a rather tiny girl shivered.

"Oh my gosh!" Wynter breathed and reached for her coat hanging neglected on the back of her chair. She wrapped it around the girl, and her family moved into action wrapping coats and blankets around the other five visitors.

"Noah, what were you thinking?" Anthony demanded.

"We had to find you. Ethan is coming."

"We got the message," Santa told him.

"We know more now," the tiny girl provided.

"So, do you want to know or not?" a second, taller girl asked with clear cut attitude that caused another guy to fight a slight turn up on one corner of his mouth.

"Who are you?" Joseph asked suspiciously.

"Uncle Joseph, this is Noah," Wynter introduced. "This is my Uncle Joseph, Uncle Israel, my Aunt Mary, and Aunt Star."

"Pleased to meet you all," Noah nodded at everyone individually. "These are my friends Lorelei, Declan, Kyson, Vivienne, and Enoch."

"Okay, but what are they all doing here?" Joseph continued to question.

"We all agree that this feud has gone on long enough, and we're here to help put a stop to it."

"And, who says that's why we're here?" Star asked with a smile that said she was clearly interested.

"Oh... um."

"That's exactly why you're all here," Santa interrupted. "I was waiting for North to get here, but... I need your help to protect the North Pole from an attack."

"An attack?" Israel echoed.

"We got word from Noah about an impending attack, but maybe it would be best if we let him tell you himself."

Noah cleared his throat nervously. "Yeah, my brother, Ethan, and a group of others are planning an attack."

"Others? You mean other South Polers like yourself?" Star quizzed.

"I do mean other South Polers, but not like us. They hold tight to the age old grudge, even though I don't personally know anyone who can even remember what the feud was originally about." Noah looked around the room from person to person. One by one each of the Clause siblings shook their head.

Star was last to respond. "Daddy, didn't know either. I asked him once."

"Really?" Wynter marveled.

"Nah, I've always been... fascinated by the feud. Daddy couldn't remember anyone ever talking about what had started the feud or even a reasonable excuse why the South Pole people are so hated."

"No one from the South Pole knows anything either," Lorelei added.

"I can't believe you had the guts to go down there," Star breathed looking at Wynter like she had hung the moon. "I wanted to. I thought about it so many times, but Daddy forbid it. After his death… it felt too much like a betrayal." Star's voice had taken on a morose undertone.

"Okay, you said they're planning an attack," Israel reined it back in. "The wards around this place are designed to keep South Polers out. You, yourself, wandered around for hours looking unsuccessfully. How would they get inside?"

Noah looked at Wynter with regret in his eyes. The pain she saw there made her want to cry for him. He kept his eyes locked on Wynter while he answered Israel, "He plans to use Wynter to get in. They were friends. We were family. He's going to use that connection against her."

"How?" Wynter whispered.

"Anyway he can."

"If he asked for your help, could you turn him down?" Lorelei asked sympathetically. "If he sounded like he was in pain… freezing to death, could you ignore him?"

Tears slid unbidden down Wynter's cheeks.

"All right, that's enough. I'm taking Wynter and Noel home," Anthony declared. "Wynter doesn't go anywhere alone. There were only two people in this house who even heard Noah calling. We have to assume that they're the only two strong enough to hear the outside perimeter." He picked Noel up out of the high chair and lead Wynter with a gentle hand on her back.

"Is that true?" Noah asked looking to Santa.

"Yeah."

"So, you're saying Ethan could get here anytime, start crying out for Wynter, and none of us can hear him but Wynter?"

"And, me."

"Unless…" Star started.

"Unless what?" Joseph pushed.

"You both previously knew Noah," Star pointed out to Santa. "What if that was what allowed you to hear him in the first place? Do you know this Ethan? Will anyone, even you, hear him?"

"We need to set up a perimeter," Mary dove into action. She turned to Mrs. Clause. "You go stay with Wynter and Noel. Take anyone else with you who can't fight." She turned an accusing eye on the six South Pole visitors.

"Don't look at us like that," Vivienne spit. "We came here to fight.

"Lorelei?" Noah asked softly.

"I..." Her face fell. "I might be more use watching the baby."

"Lorelei..."

"Don't. Just don't. I don't need you rubbing it in," she said and followed Mrs. Clause out.

Chapter Seventeen

Lorelei huffed into the house behind Mrs. Clause. Wynter was right there to ask, "What's going on up there?"

Anthony stood back from the door tossing a giggling Noel in the air above his head.

"They're setting up perimeter, and we are bunking down here," Mrs. Clause provided.

"We should be helping. I should be helping. This is all my fault. If I had never gone to the South Pole, we wouldn't be in this mess."

"We never would have met either," Anthony pointed out without missing a beat.

"I need to go help."

"You aren't going anywhere alone."

"Your aunt thinks you might be the only one who will be able to hear Ethan call. She thinks that since your dad doesn't know Ethan but he did Noah, it will prevent him from hearing Ethan," Lorelei inserted.

"Hmm, that's an interesting theory," Anthony contemplated.

"All the more reason why I should be there. I'll be the only one with any advance warning," Wynter persisted.

"I told you I won't let you go anywhere without me," Anthony told her again.

"Are you really as strong as Noah says you are?" Lorelei asked Wynter.

"I'm as strong as a Clause," Wynter answered modestly.

"She is," Anthony corrected honestly.

"I can stay here with Noel," Lorelei offered.

Wynter looked at Lorelei. She appeared nice enough and genuinely eager to help. The question was whether she was qualified or not. Wynter moved her gaze to Anthony, torn about what to do. On one hand she wanted to help, but on the other hand she wanted to stay close to Noel to protect her.

"I'll be here," Wynter's mother encouraged. "We'll guard her with our lives."

"That's right," Lorelei agreed. "If you're really as good as they say you are, then we all stand a better chance with you on the front lines."

Wynter looked again to Anthony for guidance. He gave a negligent shrug and said, "I'm with you whatever you decide."

"I'm going to leave Roscoe here too," Wynter decided.

"Roscoe?"

"Her pet bear," Anthony explained to Lorelei.

"Wow, that part was for real?"

"You and Noah must be close," Anthony observed.

"Oh, we talk. I don't know that I would call us close. He thinks I'm weak."

"I doubt that," Wynter reacted but felt the need to clarify when Lorelei appeared startled. "Noah, respects strength, and he likes to surround himself with strong people. He always has. If he considers you a friend, then he considers you a strong person. He's a protector too. If he believed you were too weak to be safe here, you can be assured he wouldn't have brought you along."

"He wanted me to stay behind, but I refused."

Wynter shook her head vehemently unsure of how to make this young girl understand. It was Anthony that spoke up. "No, it wouldn't matter to Noah. If he truly thought you were unsafe he wouldn't have taken no as an answer. He may have wanted you to stay behind to shield you from the pain, but there was no way he would let you come if you couldn't handle it."

Lorelei swallowed visibly and nodded silently. "I'll do my best."

"So, are we going out?" Anthony asked.

"Yes," Wynter breathed.

"Wynter, he was your friend. No one could blame you if you sat this one out," Anthony reminded her.

"He was your friend too. He's Noah's brother. I have no more right to sit this one out than you, less right than Noah."

"Still."

"No, it's time to choose a side. I have to choose you and Noel."

Anthony nodded without further argument and handed Noel over to Mrs. Clause. "See you later, sweet girl," he said and kissed her head.

Wynter kissed Noel's cheek and said, "I'll see you in a little while be good for Gam."

"Gam, play," Noel demanded.

"Absolutely," Mrs. Clause agreed.

Wynter watched Lorelei disappear into Noel's bedroom behind Mrs. Clause carrying Noel. Then she and Anthony slipped out the back door and locked it securely behind them. Roscoe was waiting outside the door. He probably sensed the tension and smelled the unfamiliar people.

"I want you to stay here next to the house. Don't let anyone past," Wynter instructed Roscoe. "There are strangers here. Some are nice. Others aren't. We don't know if they would hurt Noel or not, so don't take any chances. Ethan is here. He's not to be trusted. No matter what he says Roscoe, Ethan's the one who brought the group who want to hurt us."

Roscoe growled low and menacingly. The rumble vibrated through Wynter's chest giving her a warm comforting feeling that spread all the way to her toes.

Anthony scratched behind Roscoe's ears. "That's it boy. You're man of the house while I'm out. Protect our girl."

Chapter Eighteen

Back up at Santa's house, everyone was fast at work making preparations and plans. All signs of the earlier meal had been cleared away, the table was covered with maps.

"You need to stay on this side of the boundaries or be sure you have a Clause with you," Santa was saying as he moved his gaze from Noah to each of his friends in turn. "You can leave on your own, but to reenter you will need a Clause escort."

"Why don't we pair up so that there is no chance of a South Poler getting caught on the other side without a way back in?" Israel proposed.

Santa looked questioningly at Noah, who nodded his agreement.

Anthony very delicately cleared his throat and said, "Ethan is planning to target Wynter specifically. No offence but I'm not leaving Wynter with anyone. Not even you Noah."

"So? We outnumber the South Polers even with the other girl, and North will be here too. Everyone won't get paired up with a South Poler. Why shouldn't you two pair together?" Star said like it was simple everyday common sense. Maybe for someone who spent her life vampire hunting, strategizing was an everyday commonality.

"Lorelei?" Noah asked Wynter quietly.

"She's with mom and Noel."

"All right, that's settled," Santa started again.

"Uh, one more thing," Mary interrupted.

"What's that?"

"I'm dressed for travel not battle," Mary said indicating her loose sweats and sneakers.

"Right, take ten minutes and meet back in here." Everyone scattered leaving Santa alone in the kitchen with Anthony and Wynter. He pulled Wynter into his arms for a strong hug. "How are you hanging in there, baby girl?"

Wynter nodded against her father's chest but didn't say a word.

"I'm so sorry you have to go through this."

"We're going to get through this, right?"

"Of course we are."

"Without bloodshed?"

"I don't know."

"If I could make a suggestion, sir?" Anthony interjected.

"Of course, Anthony, what is it?"

"Noah is a great strategist."

Santa nodded thoughtfully. "I'll keep that in mind."

"Love you, Daddy," Wynter whispered.

"Love you too."

Noah, Declan, and Kyson were the first three back to the kitchen. "How are we going to do this?" Declan asked.

Santa's lips formed a hard, straight line. "I hear Noah is quite the strategist."

"Oh," Noah looked alarmed toward Anthony and Wynter. "That was snowball fights. It's hardly the same thing."

"He's a ranger," Kyson said in a corrective tone. "He's one of the best warriors, protectors we have."

Santa gave a single nod as if the matter had been settled. "It's time someone who had battle knowledge stepped up to the range. My family wants to look to me as the eldest, but my expertise is in spreading happiness. They're the warriors."

"Why not let one of them take lead?" Noah questioned.

"No, you know your brother. You know how the South Pole thinks. I think you'll be just right for the job."

"You suggested we split up and form a perimeter; I agree with that plan of action. What could you possible need me for?"

Santa was saved from answering when the others walked in. "Is this everyone?" he asked. "Where's Star?"

"Right here," Star announced sliding through the door in booted feet... surprisingly booted feet.

Declan let out a woof whistle, and Star shot him a flirtatious smile.

"You have got to be kidding me?" Mary groaned.

Star was dressed from the neck down in skin tight black, fur lined leather. Her black knee-high boots balanced on spike heels, and her black hair was pulled up in a French twist. The creamy porcelain skin on her face contrasted starkly with the black leather that covered every other inch of skin, and her lips were painted a shockingly bright red.

"Hey, Vivienne, think you could fight in boots like that?" Declan teased obnoxiously. Kyson gave Vivienne an all too interested look from head to toe and back up again.

"Fat chance," Vivienne shot back.

"I wouldn't mind watching you try," Kyson smiled wickedly.

"Don't hold your breath. How do you even move in that?"

"Experience honey. I've been fighting in heels longer than you've been alive."

Declan smiled stupidly and nodded his head still drinking in all that was Star. The girl certainly shined as bright as any star he had ever seen. "Who cares how she does it just so long as she does it? She's pure sex appeal in heels."

"Okay, let's focus," Santa rained them all in. He wasn't comfortable with some kid talking about his baby sister and sex in the same sentence. "We still need to split into teams and assign positions. Noah is going to set the teams up."

Noah's eyes got huge and bugged out. He took a deep breath and tried to work up his nerve to boss around a group of Clauses who possessed more magic in their pinkies than he did in his whole body and had been fighting vampires for centuries.

"Start off by telling him a little about your battle style so he can better pair you," Santa ordered his brothers and sisters.

Israel raised his hand and said, "I'll go first. I'm methodical. I like to analyze and think things through in order to take the quickest and most direct path to my goal."

That would mean he and Kyson would have the same tactical approach.

Mary went next. "I don't wait." She gave Anthony a pointed look that Noah didn't understand and continued, "Seconds count in this business, and I make the most of them. Hesitation means failure."

She sounded impulsive like Declan. Noah didn't want two impulsive thinkers together. She also sounded angry much like Vivienne, which would mean they wouldn't necessarily pair up well together. Then again it might just be that they are the only ones who can handle each other.

"I'm more easy going," Joseph spoke up. "I mean don't get me wrong. I do believe that seconds count and that you need to think through your action, but I have no desire to over think things or put myself in a rush."

What Noah heard was that Joseph thought things through, but he didn't. He took his time, but he didn't. Basically he was a walking contradiction like Enoch.

"Well, unlike my siblings, I like to fight with a certain kind of flare," Star shared.

Noah imagined that she did everything with a degree of flare or flash. He was quickly starting to think of her as a drama queen.

"I call Star!" Declan declared.

Noah ignored Declan and looked at Santa, who didn't seem inclined to share. "That just leaves you," Noah pushed.

"Me? I'm clueless. I have no fighting style, because I don't fight. I have no experience with this sort of thing."

He was nervous is what Santa wasn't saying. He needed to be paired with someone strong. Noah was pretty sure he could pair most of them up successfully, but Vivienne and Mary were going to be tough nuts to crack. They were just so angry and so violent. Noah was hesitant to put them together, but at the same time Vivienne needed a Clause to be sure she didn't get stuck outside the boundaries.

"You said there is another one of you on his way? Could you tell me about him?" Noah requested.

"We don't work together much. We can cover more ground if we spread out," Israel tried to explain.

Well, that didn't help.

"He's very much the big brother," Joseph described. "Like Israel pointed out we're all used to fighting alone. North is used to being in charge. He's very protective too."

He actually sounded perfect to pair up with Lorelei, but Noah was much happier having Lorelei where she was currently. "Okay, I think I've got it," he said.

"I don't want to be paired up with someone who is going to hold me back. I'm not working with some weak male who thinks he needs to protect me either," Mary made sure Noah understood.

"Ditto that," Vivienne seconded.

"Let me ask you two this. Do you think there is anyone here you could work with?"

The women sized each other up for a minute before saying at the same time, "Her."

"Okay, let's start there. You two can partner up, but..."

"But what?" Santa pushed.

Noah gave Vivienne a serious look. "Don't kill anyone unless absolutely necessary to your own survival."

"I think we should get that out in the open now," Joseph spoke up. "Are we fighting to kill or to capture, because there is a big difference. You fight differently when you're fighting to capture than when you are to kill."

"Capture," Wynter quickly answered.

Joseph looked to Wynter with a sympathetic nod. "All right."

"That's settled?" Noah asked. He didn't want to go into this worried that someone was out to kill his brother. Ethan was pig headed and obnoxious at times, but Noah loved him and couldn't imagine losing him.

Wynter looked to Santa and said in a shamed voice, "I want to hear them say it."

"I don't think that's too much to ask given the very personal situation to so many of us here," Santa agreed. "Anthony?"

"Ethan was my friend too. I absolutely agree."

One by one they went around the room and each person agreed they were not out to kill anyone unless it became necessary to save another. It wasn't much assurance that Ethan was safe, but it was all Noah was going to get. Ethan had put himself in this situation after all.

Chapter Nineteen

"Are you all right, dear?" Mrs. Clause asked a very anxious looking Lorelei.

"Not really. I refused to stay home, because I wanted to help. Now I'm hiding out here."

"You're helping to watch out for my granddaughter who can't protect herself."

"You don't need any help with that. I saw the fireball you slung at the crowd that night in the South Pole. None of our people could defend against that. They'll never get past you to hurt Noel. You don't need me here to protect her."

"We all have our callings."

"I know… Noah didn't want me to come at all. I've been so mad at him for suggesting I stay behind."

"It sounds like he cares for you very much."

"Yeah."

"You care for him too." It wasn't a question. Mrs. Clause could see the truth shining in Lorelei's eyes.

"I wanted to prove to him I was brave, but more than that I wanted to help. I want to put an end to the feud."

"I feel somewhat removed from the feud," Mrs. Clause mused. "Oh, I'm certainly a part of it now, but I wasn't born into it. I married into a feud that I've never really understood."

"I don't think anyone ever understood it."

"The question is what we do about it."

"Stop it?"

Mrs. Clause chuckled. "Is that a question?"

"No? I don't know. It needs to end. I just hate that it has to end violently."

"Maybe you're just the voice of reason that bunch of fighters need up there."

"But, I know the group coming after your family. They're not interested in peaceful talks. They are literally out for blood."

"That's unfortunate but sometimes necessary. I'm not usually the violent type, but when I knew Wynter was in the South Pole and thought she was in danger, to be honest, I was out for blood too. Not that I went down there to wipe out all of the South Pole people, but I knew I would hurt anyone who stood between me and my little girl."

"So, you're saying that you agree with the others?"

"To an extent, I suppose I do. Mostly I want to see this settled peacefully no matter how unlikely I think that is, but there is a very determined part of me that has every intention of hurting anyone coming in here after my granddaughter. What I'm saying is I want peace, but I'm willing to fight if I need to."

Lorelei nodded. "That's how I feel too, but how can you stand it knowing that your family is fighting up there while you hide out here?"

"That depends on your perspective. I'm not hiding out. I'm a Clause by marriage, which means my husband and daughter are much stronger than I am. They are exactly where they're supposed to be, and so am I. Noel will be very strong herself one day, but for now, she needs to be protected. I'm on protection detail not hiding. If you feel like you're hiding out, maybe you're in the wrong place."

Lorelei thought about that for a minute. Mrs. Clause didn't need her here. She was much more capable of protecting Noel than Lorelei was. Lorelei had insisted she come to the North Pole, because it meant something to her. She wanted to help. She wanted to make a stand. She wanted this stupid feud to end. This was something she needed to do. She hadn't let Noah push her out, and now she was backing herself out.

"I should have stayed to help," Lorelei admitted with defeat. "I promised to help look after Noel."

"It's not too late. I know that Wynter of all people would understand the hard choices we sometimes have to make in life." Mrs. Clause pulled out a phone, pressed a button, and put it to her ear. "Dear, I think Lorelei needs to speak with Noah right quick... Yes, I'm aware of that, but this is important."

❄ ❄ ❄

Noah had paired off Mary and Vivienne together even though he wasn't fully sold on the idea, but everyone else was paired off. They were just beginning to assign areas to each set of partners when Santa's phone started ringing.

"Yes?... We are just about to head out to set up perimeter... Fine, but make it fast." Santa held his phone out to Noah explaining, "They want to talk to you?"

They? Who would be calling Santa's phone to get in touch with Noah? "Hello?"

"Noah, I need to be there," Lorelei said desperately over the line.

"Lorelei, are you okay?"

"No I'm not; I can't hide out here like some coward. I came here for a reason, and if I don't follow through, I'll never forgive myself."

"We're getting ready to leave. I don't have time to come get you."

"I'll come to you."

"No! You don't need to be out walking around alone. Just stay there."

"I can't, Noah. Please, don't make me." She was begging, and that was Noah's undoing. He couldn't stand the idea that she was hurting, but he didn't want to see her get hurt in battle either.

"It will be safer down there," he pointed out.

"I'm coming, Noah." Lorelei was serious.

"No, just wait someone will come for you."

"I'll go get her," Vivienne offered which made Kyson squirm.

"No, no one goes anywhere alone," Noah told everyone.

"You need a Clause with you just in case too," Mary agreed. "We're partners I'll go with you."

"Fine by me," Vivienne accepted. The movement of Kyson's shoulders as his whole body relaxed was noticeable which made Declan smirk.

Noah nodded as Mary and Vivienne moved to the door. "Lorelei, stay put. Mary and Vivienne are on their way."

"Thank you, Noah," Lorelei said before hanging up.

Noah really wanted to keep Lorelei with himself so that he would know she was safe. Everyone was paired up already. She would make three anywhere Noah decided to put her, but he knew if he put her with himself and Santa she would be a distraction for him. He would neglect protecting Santa in lieu of protecting Lorelei, and he wouldn't want to let her go when North got here. Joseph had said that North was the overprotective type.

That was exactly the type he needed paired with Lorelei
assuming of course that he could work with a
South Poler.

"When North gets here, do any of you think he
would have a problem working with a South Poler?"
Noah asked.

"You have to admit it is an odd situation, joining
forces with a South Poler to stop South Polers,"
Israel said.

"But is he safe to work with?" Enoch pushed.

"Sure he is," Star said. "He'll protect anyone. That's
what he does."

"All right… Wynter can I put Lorelei with you and
Anthony just until North gets here?"

"That's fine."

Chapter Twenty

"So, you're really from the South Pole?" Star asked Declan later as they surveyed the horizon.

"Born and raised. This is my first trip outside the South Pole. It must be amazing to travel all over the world the way you do."

"It is. I meet all sorts of fascinating people, and the shopping is magnificent. What about you though? You have a place to call home. You're surrounded by friends and family."

"You don't have a place you can call home?" Declan asked morosely.

"Just a long string of hotels. Don't feel too badly for me though. I'm living the high life; five star hotels, fine foods, fine clothes, and nightlife filled with action."

"I bet it is. You any good at vampire hunting?"

"I do all right."

"I can't wait to see if you make battle look as good as you do everything else," Declan smiled.

"Well, keep your eyes open, and you just might get your wish. Tell me about the South Pole."

"One word, cold."

Star giggled and gave Declan a playful shove. "You're funny."

Declan couldn't stop a goofy grin from taking over his entire face when Star flirted like that. She was beautiful. Her dark hair didn't match with what Declan typically thought of as a Clause trait, but that sparkle in her eyes was definitely Clause through and through. She wasn't tall, but she was curved in all the right places. That skin tight leather she was wearing didn't do anything to hide all those delicious curves either.

"The South Pole is not much different from here, just a little more crowded."

"Sounds like the humans."

"I would love to travel the way you do and see the world," Declan admitted. "Were you serious back there about wanting to visit the South Pole?"

"Yeah."

"Maybe after all this is over, you can come down for a visit."

"That would be nice."

"Sure, I can show you around," Declan offered.

"What is going on here?" a tall broad man asked as he stepped into sight. He was clearly a Clause. Declan knew without Star saying anything that this must have been her brother North. He had that same sparkle to his eyes that Star had.

"North! You made it!" Star enthused.

"Yeah, does somebody want to tell me what's going on, and why there's a bunch of strangers wandering around outside the North Pole?"

"They're from the South Pole," Declan filled in.

"This is Declan; he's from the South Pole too, but he came with his friends to warn us. How did you know Wynter again?" Star tried to remember.

"Actually, I don't. Noah is the one who knows Wynter, and Noah is one of my best friends. That's only part of why I'm here. There are six of us here who all think this feud needs to end. We're here to do whatever we have to do to be sure that happens."

"Where are the other five, and why are you alone with my sister talking about taking her to the South Pole?" Declan had made a seriously poor first impression with Star's brother.

"That was a private conversation, North. Don't be such a fuddy duddy. We all split up. The South Polers can't get past the wards without one of us. Anthony wouldn't let Wynter go without him though. It's a little overprotective if you ask me. He must have taken a page out of your book."

North rolled his eyes at the snide comment.

"There's another girl, Lorelei with Wynter and Anthony. She's going to be paired with you as soon as you get here. We've all split up to cover the perimeter."

"Did you see how many were out there or which direction they were coming from?" Declan inquired.

"The last I saw they were at the south east corner, but I didn't get a clear count."

"No one has," Declan sighed, "but we think there could be as many as twenty."

"Which way are Anthony and Wynter?"

"They are more to the north from here," Star answered.

"Right, you two be careful." North hugged Star before starting off to the north, and Declan couldn't resist a laugh.

"What's so funny?" Star wanted to know.

"You just sent your brother, North to the north."

❄ ❄ ❄

"How you holding in there?" Anthony asked Lorelei.

"I'm fine. It's a little too quiet. It's sort of eerie just waiting for an avalanche, you know?"

"That's the way I felt hiding who I was from everyone while I was in the South Pole," Wynter agreed.

"Is it true that nobody knew the truth?"

"Well, Anthony figured me out pretty quick. He has a bad habit of lurking."

"I do not lurk," Anthony protested.

"He was lurking," Wynter assured Lorelei. "He caught me using more magic than I should have had access to and knew right away."

"Is that when you knew you loved her?" Lorelei asked Anthony.

"No, my love for Wynter was a little more subtle than that. What I did know right away was that I wanted her help."

"What about you? When did you first realize you love Noah?" Wynter asked not so subtly.

"Oh... I... What?"

"I didn't realize the two of you were together. Noah didn't say anything," Anthony observed.

"We aren't. I mean we've never..."

"But you love him, right?" Wynter continued to pry.

"I... well... How did you know?" Lorelei sighed.

"The way you look at him, it's the way I've watched my mother look at my father all my life. I may not have always agreed with them, but I've never doubted their love for each other."

"That's really sweet."

"It is. You must be Lorelei. I'm North," Uncle North introduced startling Lorelei with his sudden appearance.

Uncle North was an expert at sudden appearances. Wynter couldn't remember a single time in life that Uncle North's appearance hadn't been sudden.

"Oh, hi," Lorelei greeted shyly.

"Which way should we move?" North asked.

"Dad is stationed to the west with Noah. They said for you to head that way when you get here."

"Right, let's go Lorelei. You two be careful."

Anthony watched North disappear out of sight before he commented, "North gets straight to business, huh?"

"Yeah, he's serious like Israel gets at times."

"I guess spending a lifetime hunting vampires would make most people serious. It's a serious business after all."

"I don't understand how you can be so calm and understanding about all this," Wynter told him honestly.

"Because I understand. The vampires I knew were monsters."

"What about you? You weren't a monster."

"Wasn't I?"

"No."

"Why not? What made me so different?" Anthony challenged.

"You didn't want to be like the others. You didn't want to be a vampire. You didn't want to be a monster."

"I didn't want to be like the others, because, like them I craved blood."

"But, you resisted."

"Not very well at times. I was running away if you recall. I believe the point, whether I was a monster or not, is that the others were and are monsters."

"Doesn't it still make things awkward for you, though, knowing that they hunt what you were?"

"Aren't you the one who just said I was different because I didn't want to be a blood sucking, life stealing vampire? I've never seen another vampire who didn't want to be a vampire."

"So that makes it okay to hunt them?"

"You don't know what they're like. They don't care who they hurt as long as they get the blood they crave. I didn't ask to be turned. How many more like me are there out there?"

"Exactly, what if they are killing people who only wanted a second chance?"

"Wynter, you're not listening to what I'm telling you. I've never met anyone else who didn't want to be a vampire. Whether they asked to be changed or not, they were. It changes you; it just does something to you."

"Then why did you not want it?"

"I don't know, but Wynter what I'm trying to get through to you is that it isn't normal. Even if it was to ever happen again, that didn't stop me from being a monster. I still craved blood. I couldn't fight it except to remove myself from the situation, far removed. I deserved to be hunted. The vampires that your aunts and uncles are hunting deserve it too, and if Mary had caught and killed me, it was nothing less than I deserved."

"Anthony, don't say that!" Wynter's eyes were tearing up, and Anthony pulled her against his chest.

"I'm sorry, Wynter. Don't cry. It's all different now. I'm not that person anymore, and maybe..."

Wynter pulled back. Her spine straightened, and her whole body went on alert as she looked around suspiciously.

Anthony scanned the horizon but couldn't see anything out of the ordinary. There was nothing there that he could see, but that didn't mean there wasn't anything there, or anyone. "What is it? Do you hear something?"

"I don't know. Maybe..."

<h2 style="text-align:center">Chapter Twenty-One</h2>

"Do you really think this is going to work?" Aldon asked.

He was always questioning Ethan. He was the weak link. This was going to work, and if Aldon wasn't prepared to do whatever it takes, then he should have stayed home. He wasn't much better than Noah. Thinking of Noah, that traitor, Ethan hadn't seen him anywhere yet. Noah and his friends disappeared no doubt headed up here. He was here somewhere, and when Ethan found him, he was going to pummel that kid and send him home where he belonged.

When was that fool kid going to grow up? Wynter was a Clause. Nothing was going to change that. She lied to them and nearly got them all killed. Then she ran home like a good little Clause. Not that Ethan cared, he was glad she went back where she belonged.

"It will work," Ethan ground out in frustration. It wasn't Aldon's fault; Ethan always seemed to be mad these days "I was just asking. It seems sort of farfetched that she will be able to hear us when we can't see anything, and why would she let us in?"

"Because I'm going to ask nicely."

Parker chuckled darkly. "She's a Clause. Asking nicely won't make a difference. The Clauses don't understand nice. Not a good one in the whole bunch."

Scenes from Ethan's time with Wynter flashed through his mind, but it was all tainted now with lies and deception. She had lied to him from the very beginning. How she must have laughed at him, the very idea of him teaching her magic, and like a fool he fell for it. He had spent hours training her, and the whole time she had been mocking him. Poking fun at the weakling. They'd see who the weakling was in the end. Ethan wasn't that stupid little boy any longer.

The most pathetic part wasn't that he thought he was teaching her magic but that he had actually believed she was his friend. No, not just friends, he had believed they were good friends, close friends, best friends, the kind

of friends who could tell each other anything. She didn't tell him the most important thing about herself, the very essence of what made her who she was. She never told him who she really was. The best friend he ever had never even told him the most basic information about herself. She didn't trust him enough to give him her real name.

Guess, some things never change. No one trusts him now, not really. They'll trust him to a certain extent to lead a party against the Clauses, because he more than anyone has reason to hate them. That is as far as it goes. They don't confide in him, and they certainly don't give him the chance to confide in them. No one asks how things are going or shares everyday nuances with him. They don't hang out on the weekends. He has no friends anymore, no real friends.

Poor Noah was too young and naive to understand. He couldn't help getting brainwashed, but Ethan, he was old enough to understand. Ethan should have known better. Ethan shouldn't have been deceived. Noah had his whole life ahead of him until Ethan allowed him to get sucked in by that evil Clause child. At least that was what everyone said. They might not have said it to his face, but they said it all right, when they thought he wasn't listening.

They just don't get it. They didn't hear all her pretty lies. They didn't know how easy it was to believe her, how much you wanted to believe her. Even his parents loved her… thought they loved her…

The others would probably trust Ethan's lead more if Dad would follow through, but the man was all talk. Oh, he talked a good game about how he hated the Clauses and Wynter most of all for her deception, but when it came to doing something about it, you could count him out. That's why he wasn't here now. He talked like he was coming. He even helped with the planning but had a dozen different excuses why he couldn't come along.

What was she doing in the South Pole anyway? She didn't belong there. What did she do while she was there? That was a question that still plagued the minds of so many. Noah would say she did nothing, but that is a lie, just like all the other lies she told.

She turned Ethan's life upside down. She ruined his life, and he bet she did a lot more than what anybody knew. What did she do with all that time he and Noah were in school? She had to have been doing something, and being that she is a Clause, she was inevitably up to no good.

Ethan thought back to the night Mrs. Clause came looking for Wynter. That fireball was freaking huge! It was enough to kill dozens at once. Everyone gathered there in the middle of the night, startled out of their beds would have been rendered to nothing but ash. Then Wynter tried to play the hero. Let Noah believe that act if he wanted. Ethan sure didn't. No, that was all a well planned act. Wynter went back home to the North Pole without fuss, didn't she? Good cop, bad cop was all that was, a public scene.

Now here they were narrowing in on the North Pole to return the favor. Ethan was glad Noah had made the trip. Maybe he'd come to his senses and see the Clauses for who they really are, enact a little justice of his own.

"Isn't that right, Ethan?" Parker's voice broke through Ethan's thoughts.

"Isn't what right," he barked.

"All that stuff about the Clauses being evil incarnate and all?"

"Course it is. Why'd you have to ask? Come on. Let's keep moving. We've got to be getting close."

"How do you even know where we're going?" Aldon asked.

There Aldon went questioning Ethan's every move again. Yeah, well, no one asked him to come along. He volunteered for this same as everyone else, and Ethan didn't need him questioning every step they took. "Shut up, Aldon, and don't be stupid."

The truth was Aldon wasn't as stupid as Ethan pretended, though. Ethan didn't know much about what he was doing. He knew from other people stupid enough to lead expeditions to the North Pole that there were magical wards around it and that no one had ever found a weak link in the magic. Not that any South Poler would be a match for the weakest North Pole magic.

He also knew they hadn't seen Noah anywhere, which meant he and his little friends were already inside, so that meant it was possible for South Polers to get inside the North Pole. The only question was how, and Ethan was going to do whatever it took to find out, even if that meant letting Wynter believe she could still control him.

They had no way of seeing what was on the other side of the magical wards. All they could do was take a chance and hope they got lucky. Here was as good a place as any, so after another hour Ethan stopped to start the next part of their plan. This was the part he dreaded, because he was going to look like an idiot. It didn't matter that the others knew exactly what he was doing and all had agreed to go along with it, he was still going to look ridiculous and worthless.

"Wynter?" Ethan called into the white snowy abyss. Her name felt familiar on his lips despite the fact that he barely uttered the name these days. Ethan didn't dare turn back to see the looks of bewilderment he was no doubt receiving. Instead, he called a little louder, "Wynter?"

After a couple minutes, Aldon said, "This isn't going to work. I told you-"

"Shut up, Aldon! I'm telling you this will work," Ethan screamed. Then he cupped his hands around his mouth and screamed Wynter's name for a third time. There was no response, but Ethan didn't let that stop him. He took a deep breath and continued, "Wynter, can we talk? I miss you. I miss my friend..."

Chapter Twenty-Two

Wynter heard her name again a little louder this time and knew she wasn't imagining things. "Anthony," she whispered and latched onto his forearm for support.

"WYNTER!" This time her name was loud and clear. It was definitely Ethan's voice. "Wynter, can we talk? I miss you. I miss my friend." It was like hearing him call her name had tuned her into his frequency somehow. She could hear him as clear as if he were standing right next to her.

"He said he wants to talk, that he misses me."

"It's a trick," Anthony reminded her.

"I know."

"Wynter, can you hear me? It's cold out here. I just want to see you one more time. There are so many things we left unsaid," Ethan said.

"Don't listen to him," Anthony warned.

"Wynter… Wynter?"

Anthony looked scared. Wynter didn't know what emotions he was seeing play across her face, but whatever it was, he didn't like what he was seeing.

"SANTA, NORTH EAST CORNER OF THE PERIMETER!" Anthony's voice boomed across the sky as if on a PA system.

Ethan chuckled, and Wynter heard him whisper to his comrades, "Well, we know two things now. She can hear me, and the vampire has Clause magic."

"He's not alone."

"We knew he wouldn't be. Your dad is coming just hang on," Anthony said seconds before Santa appeared with Noah wrapped around him like a living hug.

"What's going on?" Santa inquired.

"They're here," Anthony answered.

"Can you hear him?" Noah asked Wynter.

"Yes," she whispered.

"Can he hear you?"

"I-I don't know. Ethan?" Wynter tentatively called.

"Hey, Wynter, there you are. So, you can hear me?"

"Yes." She wasn't sure if she was answering Ethan or Noah, but at this point it didn't really matter.

"Okay, listen to me, Wynter," Noah instructed. "You know him. He wasn't above using underhanded tricks to win a snowball fight, and that was just a game. Don't put it past him to use any dirty trick in the book. Don't fall for it."

"Noah is missing. Is he in there with you?" Ethan asked.

Wynter stood frozen unanswering.

"It would make me feel better to know he was safe with you... It would make me feel better to know you are safe. Are you safe, Wynter?"

Still she didn't answer.

"Is Anthony with you? Is there anyone there with you to keep you safe?"

"Wynter, baby, what's going on?" Anthony asked.

Wynter shook her head afraid to speak for fear Ethan would hear every word.

"Are you alone like me? I spend most of my time alone since you left… It's hard to keep friends when you were friends with the Clause… you know?"

"No!" the whispered gasp escaped her lips before she realized what she had done.

"Yeah… that's sort of why I'm here. I need a friend… I need you."

"Baby, don't listen to him! Wynter, look at me! Wynter!" Anthony shook her by her shoulders until she focused on his face.

Tears washed down Wynter's face as she cried, "He's hurting."

"It's a trick," Noah quickly reacted, but it was too late.

Ethan had been Wynter's first real friend, and she couldn't abandon him. Wynter closed her eyes, and when she opened them she was standing face to face with Ethan.

"WYNTER," Anthony bellowed as he grasped nothing but air where Wynter had once been. The sound unhindered by the wind.

Wynter threw herself at Ethan and hugged him as tight and close as she could get. "I'm so sorry, Ethan. I wanted to tell you. Every day, I wanted to tell you, but I was just so scared."

"Scared?"

"Get your hands off her!" Wynter lifted her head just enough to see what was going on. Anthony stood only feet away from them. His arm was cocked back ready to throw the lightning bolt that hovered in his fist crackling loudly with electricity.

Wynter spun around inside Ethan's arms to face Anthony. "Anthony! What in the world are you doing?"

She forgot all about the weapon in Anthony's hand when the hard, cold steel of a weapon pressed against her throat.

"I wouldn't do that if I were you," Ethan threatened. "Where are the others?"

"Waiting for you."

"And, my brother?"

"Same."

"Then let's not keep them waiting."

"I'm only a Clause by marriage. I'm not strong enough to carry you all inside at once."

Wynter could hear the lie in Anthony's voice. He might have only been a Clause by marriage, but he was set to be the next Santa and nature knew that.

"That bolt in your hand says otherwise. I think I'll take my chances."

Wynter at last took the time to take in her surroundings. There were only fourteen of them. Wynter knew their own number nearly matched that. "Ethan, you don't have to do this."

"Shut up, Wynter. Did you really think I wanted to be friends with you?" Ethan spit as he dug the knife deeper. The bite of the blade stung causing Wynter to gasp.

"Ethan, stop," Anthony demanded. "I don't want to kill you, but I will. For her, I will."

"Ethan, please," Wynter tried again.

"I said shut up!" He started to tighten the blade again. This time Wynter could feel warm, wet blood trickle down her neck and underneath her coat.

"All right, all right, you want inside, I'll take you."

"Anthony, no!"

"I have to. I can't let him hurt you. How many of you need inside?"

"All fourteen of us and you and Wynter, of course. Think you can handle that?"

Anthony dropped the lightning bolt. It popped and sizzled on the ground as it melted through the snow leaving a deep trench.

"I can," Anthony said in a defeated tone.

Wynter closed her eyes and said a prayer that her dad and Noah were somehow ready for what was coming their way.

"What is this?" asked a voice that Wynter didn't recognize.

She opened her eyes as Ethan drug her around in a desperate circle. All around them they were surrounded by a tight ring of six Clauses and six South Polers.

"Put the knife down, Ethan. There's been enough fighting," Noah said.

Ethan removed the knife from Wynter's neck and threw her to the ground. Before Wynter could pick herself up, Anthony was there with his hand on her throat where the knife had cut. She could literally feel the skin knitting itself back together.

The clicking of a readying gun drew Wynter's attention to a man who looked ravenous with murder in his eyes, and his gun was pointed directly at Santa. Vivienne narrowed her eyes and held in front of her a large knife meant for hunting and said in a chillingly calm voice, "You don't want to give me a reason."

The man didn't pay Vivienne any attention if he could hear her at all. He fired the gun. Then three things happened at once. Aunt Mary reached her arm toward the bullet speeding through the air causing it to explode in midair. Lorelei reached her arm toward the gun and followed it as it was ripped from the man's hand and went sailing straight up into the air, and with blurringly fast movements, Vivienne stepped forward and sliced cleanly into the man's arm leaving it dangling uselessly by his side.

After that, chaos ensued as fists flew, magic whirled, guns fired, and knives swiped.

Noah tried to put himself between Santa and everyone else since the idiots had just shown their hand. Clearly Santa was their main target, at least for most of the group. Some of the group was no doubt disappointed not to see Mrs. Clause in order to enact a little revenge for her fireball, and then there was Ethan. Ethan was here for one person and one person alone, Wynter, but

Anthony was going to have to protect her. Noah had his hands full protecting Santa.

The two biggest, burliest, meanest looking guys began advancing on Noah looking for a way around him. Noah didn't have nearly the size these two did, but ranger training wasn't for the faint of heart. He was strong and smart. The men looked vaguely familiar, but Noah couldn't place them. They were older than himself or Ethan.

"Santa stay behind me, and we'll keep you out of the fight for as long as we can," Noah suggested.

Santa didn't respond, but Noah assumed that the big guy heard all the same. While one man was distracted looking around Noah to Santa. Noah flicked his wrist and snow flew from the other man's side with a whoosh and came down on top of the first man like an avalanche.

With the first man temporarily detained, Noah focused his attention on the next man who was no longer distracted. The man lunged. The momentum of the larger man's weight took them both to the ground with Noah on bottom. He bucked and rolled quickly placing himself on top. He crossed his arms over the man's neck and began applying pressure. The man continued to punch, kick, buck, and generally fight back anyway he could; however caught in the front choke hold, the man could not breathe. His fight slowly tapered until he was too weak to fight back, and eventually he passed out.

Noah turned his attention back to the first man who by now had dug his way out of the snow and was aiming a gun in Santa's direction. Santa's arms were raised ready to defend and attack. Noah was going to save him the trouble. He raised his arm high into the air ripping the gun from the man's hand and up out of reach.

The man watched the gun float in midair as Noah slowly disassembled it magically. "What? How?" the man stuttered looking back and forth between the gun and Noah.

Noah still had his eyes glued to the man clearly bewildered by the fact that Noah could magically disassemble a gun without even looking. Piece by piece the gun fell to the ground with a thud. Finally the man decided that Noah was the bigger threat. He turned to Noah, tucked his head, and proceeded to charge like an angry rhino. Noah jumped into the air and floated there easily as he levitated his own weight.

The man stumbled and tripped when he realized he had missed his mark. He rolled on the ground until he could see Noah floating six feet above the ground. "What are you?"

Noah deemed that the question wasn't worth an answer, so he ignored it and lowered himself back to the ground. Then with an outstretched hand he motioned the man to come again.

Chapter Twenty-Three

Lorelei couldn't believe that she had just disarmed the man aiming a gun at Santa Clause. The whole situation was surreal. If someone had asked her a year ago if she could disarm a fully grown man, she would have laughed in their face, but here she was. She was brave. She was courageous, and she was fast. Too bad the man she had disarmed was fast as well.

He spun away from Vivienne with his right arm hanging limply at his side. Vivienne looked like she had problems of her own. This guy was Lorelei's problem.

"You're bleeding," North blandly told the man. That was when Lorelei remembered that North, thankfully, was still standing next to her. They had been paired together, and he seemed to take his job extremely seriously.

The man didn't pay North any attention. He simply looked past North and snarled at Lorelei, "Didn't your daddy ever tell you not to take a man's gun, little girl?"

"Didn't your daddy ever tell you real men don't threaten girls?" North responded as if the man had been addressing him all along.

"And, just who are you?"

"I'm North."

"You Clauses are so arrogant, think you're better than everyone else."

"That's not entirely true. We think we're better than the monsters we hunt. Are you a monster that needs hunting?"

The man growled and hurtled forward. North was cool, calm, and collected, but not Lorelei. She panicked forcing a tidal wave of magic out into space and squeezed her eyes shut tight. She wasn't even sure what her magical intent had been or if it had done anything at all until she opened her eyes and saw the man floating in midair.

"Not my style, but very efficient," North remarked. "Are we shooting to kill, maim, or capture?"

"Capture," Lorelei answered in relief.

"I'm going to hunt you down when I get out of this. You're dead," the man spit angrily at Lorelei.

"Maybe we could maim him just a little first," she squeaked.

North just chuckled. "I like you. You remind me of my daughter." Then he pointed at the air above the man's dangling arms, and a pair of handcuffs appeared out of nowhere.

Lorelei decided that she like North too.

❄ ❄ ❄

Joseph stood stock still watching the so called attacker watch Enoch and himself. What was this guy waiting on? "Are you ready?" Joseph asked even though it sounded like an awfully stupid question.

The man's eyes flickered back and forth between Joseph and Enoch. He looked like a caged animal who just realized this was his last meal.

"Maybe the question he's asking himself is if we are ready," Enoch purposed.

"Could be, but I bet he's been getting ready for this day for a long time."

"Probably, but how long have we been preparing our counter attack?"

"It could be a few days. It could be a few centuries."

"But then again, we do have our own lives to tend."

"True, but a big portion of my life is fighting," Joseph pointed out without cracking a smile.

"I guess in that case there's only one question he should be worried about right now... I think it was Clint Eastwood who said, 'Do you feel lucky?'"

The man let out a frustrated and terrified cry and turned in retreat.

"Yeehaw," Joseph yipped.

Enoch spared a glance at Joseph and saw the man swinging a lasso that Enoch swore wasn't there two seconds ago. Joseph threw. The lasso flew through the air and slid easily over the fleeing man's head and shoulders. once the man fell to the ground, Enoch wasted no time securing the man with the rope Joseph had so graciously provided.

"That was fun. This capture over kill thing has its rewards. What is it you do for a living?" Joseph asked Enoch.

"Lawyer."

"Wow. Well, you ever need a break, look me up. We'll go hunting together sometime."

"By hunting you mean vampires?"

"I mean monsters who wouldn't think twice about killing you if your blood could sustain them."

"I'll keep it in mind, you know, if things get too boring."

"Heads up," Joseph warned pointing over Enoch's left shoulder.

Enoch turned just in time to see a second attacker charging. Enoch stepped to the side and stuck a stiff arm out in front of the charging man. The guy hit Enoch's arm full on knocking the wind out of him and causing him to fall to his butt in the snow.

"Looks cold, doesn't he," Enoch smirked.

"Let's warm him up," Joseph replied as the snow around the attacker began to melt into a slushy bubbling mess.

The man jumped to his feet with a grunt, and Enoch couldn't help doubling over with laughter. "You Clauses aren't half bad."

"Same to you, South Poler. Shall we?" Joseph handed Enoch a zip tie, and Enoch secured the man's feet while Joseph secured the man's arms.

❄ ❄ ❄

"Not too pretty, is he?" Star said about the man standing only a yard in front of her.

The man clearly hadn't shaved in at least a week. Honestly, Declan wasn't sure what sort of grooming the man had done at all, if any. He was dirty and unkept to put it kindly.

"Don't judge us all by this one foul specimen," Declan winked.

"Oh, I wouldn't dream of it. You mind if I do the honors?"

"Please, go right ahead." Did he mind? He couldn't wait! He had enjoyed Star's outlandish outfit up to now, but he was anxious to see her fight in it. Once again Star didn't disappoint.

Star and the dirty man circled around. Neither turned their back to the other, and neither took their eyes off the other. Star moved gracefully like a wildcat on the prowl. How she navigated the snow in those heels was a mystery, but how she did so in a way that made Declan's blood boil was nothing short of a miracle.

The man wore a grimace, but Star was still smiling. Her teeth were as white as the snow, and they gleamed just inside her rose red lips. She was so beautiful... and deadly.

At last the man made his first move running at Star. She jumped inhumanly high and landed agilely on her feet behind the man. He looked about dazed. Star used the opportunity to fire off at the man's back what appeared to be bright pink... sparkle. The man jolted forward. He fell to his knees but quickly recovered.

The circling began again. The man took an experimental step forward. Star didn't move away. The man took another step forward and sneered, "I'm going to have fun getting my hands on you, sweet cheeks."

Declan's blood burned hot again but for an entirely different reason this time. Star put her hand up like a stop sign when the man went to move in, and she sing-songed, "Ah, ah, ah, boys on the naughty list don't get new toys for Christmas."

Then a load of coal fell from thin air on top of the man, burying him. Declan smiled in victory, but Star merely kept her eyes on the coal pile and leaned into a crouch.

Before Declan could take in his next breath, coal exploded in all directions, and the vial man tackled Star. She wrapped her legs around the man, and they rolled across the snow each one vying for the upper hand. Declan followed behind the scuffle looking for an opening to knock this guy into next week for talking to Star the way he did and daring to touch a single hair on her head.

Just when Declan was about to wrap his hands around the unwashed man, an explosion of red glitter threw him back several feet. He jumped back swiftly to his feet. "Star!"

Star stood up calmly, sinuously and started brushing glitter off her leather outfit. Declan sighed as he watched Star's hands gently caressing her unmarred body.

"Could you... ewe," Star requested holding out a pair of pink cuffs in the man's general direction. She didn't look down as if she couldn't stand the sight of all that filth.

Pink, it was perfect. "It would be my pleasure."

The man was lying unconscious on the snow. He was covered in a fine layer of red glitter, and now he was accessorized with a pair of pink cuffs. When Declan finished securing the man, he turned back to Star and said, "That was by far the sexiest thing I have ever seen!"

"I'm just getting warmed up," Star replied stalking closer with every word.

❋ ❋ ❋

There were two guys advancing on Kyson and Israel. They both looked red in the eyes and long in the tooth. There was an undeniable glint of determination in their eyes. There was no telling how long these two had been building up their hatred of all things North Pole including the Clauses.

Kyson recognized one of the two guys, not really a friend of the family, but he was still someone his family knew. He must have recognized Kyson as well as he zeroed in on Kyson. If looks could kill then the laser beams shooting from the man's eyes and drilling a hole in Kyson's skull would have left Kyson dead on the spot.

"It's time someone taught you a lesson, boy," the man said in a gravelly voice. Then he raised his arms in front of him, and the ground beneath Kyson's feet literally began to quake then lift away from the earth.

This man was strong, stronger than Kyson. It was very uncommon for a South Poler's magic to be strong enough to lift a full grown person, but Kyson had one thing the man didn't... a level head with a clear conscious.

Kyson didn't lose his head. He kept balance and rode the ice patch as high as the man intended, or as high as the man could muster. Kyson wasn't sure. It was only a couple feet off the ground, but it left Kyson looking down on the man. He jumped down surprising the man and pushing him underneath the patch of ice. Because the man had lost his concentration when Kyson jumped, the ice came back down to earth quickly, right on top of the man's head.

The man crumpled easily to the ground. For a moment, Kyson was afraid he had killed the man, but he sat up and shook his head as if trying to shake away his own confusion. Then he fixed his glare once more on Kyson. If he wasn't mad before, he was mad now.

Israel could see Kyson out of the corner of his eye holding his own, which was good. Israel had his own problem to deal with right now. The second man was inching closer. There were multiple ways that Israel could easily kill the man right now. He would be much easier to kill than a vampire, being that they weren't nearly as strong as vampires. Israel was used to killing too. That's what you did with vampires. You didn't pop them on the nose and tell them they'd been bad. It wasn't in their nature to be better.

Anthony had been the one exception to that rule that Israel had ever come across. If he had always been destined to be the next Santa, though, it made sense that he would be the exception to many rules.

Right now Israel needed to focus on disarming not killing. It shouldn't be that hard. The man was still inching ever closer; he was only feet away now. Israel built a cylindrical cage around the man thinking to hold him prisoner, but the man lifted the cage over his head and flung it away.

The problem was that Israel knew little to nothing about South Pole magic. He had never had encounters with South Polers or ever been the least bit curious about them. They lived in their world, and he lived in his, never the two to meet. Well, they were meeting now with a violent beginning.

The man used magic to launch a large snowball aimed directly at Israel's head. A snowball, really? What was with this guy? Did he really know so little about Clause magic that he thought Israel could be stopped with a snowball? All it took was a single thought and the snowball melted and splashed to ground. They were standing close enough together that they both got drenched from the spray.

The last thing Israel was going to do was stand out here soaking wet to die of hypothermia. A quick gust of heat and his clothes were dry again. He thought about Wynter and the promise he had made to her not to kill the South Polers, so with a roll of his eyes he dried his opponent's clothes too.

The man looked taken aback at first, frightened. Israel couldn't blame him. If one of the vampires had done something that appeared to help him, Israel would be suspicious and more so on alert.

Next the man pulled a knife from his belt and lobbed it at Israel's chest. Nope. There would be none of that today. Israel lifted his hand and aimed a flash of orange magic at the knife causing it to explode into tiny harmless pieces that stung as they hit both men.

The man roared in frustration. He pulled another weapon then another. One by one Israel disarmed the man. With magic flashing all around them, it looked like they were caught in the middle of a fireworks extravaganza. Blues and greens exploded and showered down on top of them. Yellow streaked across the sky like lightning. Purples and reds circled around like a strobe light. Oranges and whites twinkled all around like strings of Christmas lights.

Eventually the man stood huffing and puffing and completely disarmed.

Kyson's attacker glared at him with murder in his eyes. He clearly wanted Kyson dead, and Kyson thought about his family. If they could see him now, if they could watch this scene unfold, whose side would they be on? Would they want to see Kyson dead as well… or imprisoned… or maybe just punished and brought back home where they could keep a closer eye on him?

"You're a disgrace," they guy told Kyson.

"I'm not the one who stands here ready to shed innocent blood."

"Innocent, hah, don't make me laugh, boy. They're Clauses."

"Who have they hurt?"

The man narrowed his eyes but gave no other reaction.

"Who have I hurt? You look at me now as if you'd like to see me dead. Would you kill me? Would you tell my family what happened here today and how I died by your hands?"

This gave the man pause but only for a minute. "This is war."

"Then why have you declared war? The Clauses certainly haven't. They've shown me more kindness in the short time since we got here than many South Polers have shown me in a lifetime."

"It was war as soon as Mrs. Clause flew down South."

"All she wanted was her daughter, her only child. What lengths would you go to if you feared for the life of one of your children?" Kyson couldn't remember if the man had any children or not, but he prayed that the man did.

The man's shoulders slumped. "I suppose I would have done the same thing… but that don't make it right."

"No, it doesn't, but parents have been making wrong choices for all the right reasons since Cain and Able."

"You've given this a lot of thought, huh, boy."

"I have."

The man studied Kyson for a minute. "I guess it was hard to go against your family the way you are."

"It was."

"Let me ask you this, boy. Were you scared coming all the way up here to meet the Clauses and go against your own kind?"

"Terrified."

"I guess in that case, I can respect you doing what you thought was right."

"But, can you call all this off?" Kyson asked.

"That's not my call, but I can give you my word for my own doing."

"Now what?" Israel called his attacker out.

The man didn't answer but lunged straight for Israel's throat instead. It wasn't anything a thousand vampires hadn't tried before, but it was a weaker attack this time. Israel tucked his chin and wrapped his left hand around the man's left wrist. Then simultaneously he kicked the man with his knee and thrust the heel of his right hand into the man's nose.

The man immediately dropped to the ground curled in a fetal position and clutching at his bloody nose. Israel resorted to a more humane means of capture and produced a pair of cuffs with which to cuff the man.

❄ ❄ ❄

Only one man came toward Vivienne and Mary, which Vivienne thought mores the pity. This lone man, however, looked at the girls like he could have been president and founder of the he man women haters club.

That was something that Vivienne couldn't stand. With three much older brothers she was always being left out when she was younger, because she was too weak. Never again. She could keep up with any of the boys, and she'd have fun doing it.

The man grinned and motioned for them to come forward like he wanted them both to attack him at once. "Was that supposed to be an invitation?" Vivienne asked Mary.

"I think so. I hate to disappoint him, but he's not my type."

Vivienne burst out laughing at Mary's joke. This girl was too much fun! "I do hope we stay in touch when this is all over."

"Definitely," Mary answered thinking that Vivienne would be fun to hunt with. "We could plan a weekend hunting trip."

"As in hunting vampires? That would involve a lot of fighting, right? I'm so there!"

"You girls are nuts," the man said inching backwards.

Vivienne looked at Mary. Mary looked at Vivienne, and it was like the two women could read each other's mind. Mary winked then disappeared only to reappear behind the man as Vivienne closed in on him from the front.

"You're not recanting that romantic invitation, now are you?" Vivienne asked.

Mary pushed the man from behind sending him toppling into Vivienne.

"You're a long way from home," Vivienne commented as she pushed the guy back into Mary.

"I heard you were here to hurt my family," Mary added pushing him again.

"I heard the same thing." Another push.

"I don't like it when people threaten my family." Push.

"I don't like it when innocent people get threatened." Push.

"Stop it. Stop it," the man begged.

"He's not very tough for a man who came here to wipe out an entire family," Mary pointed out pushing him again.

"You know what they say; the bigger they are the harder they fall." Push.

"Yeah, but I promised Wynter not to kill the guy." Push.

The guy whimpered.

"Why'd we get stuck with the coward?" Vivienne asked.

"It takes a coward to attack women."

"It's a shame the coward didn't realize what kind of women he was attacking."

"What do we do with him now?"

"Put him out of his misery," Vivienne suggested.

"No, please, no," the man begged, but it was too late.

Mary hit him over the head, knocking him out cold.

Vivienne's eyes widened as she looked over Mary's shoulder. "Hey, there's two getting away!"

Mary turned to see one man disappear over the horizon and a second close on his heels, heading deeper into the North Pole, closer to Mrs. Clause and Noel. Both Mary and Vivienne took off running through the deep snow after the two men who were getting away.

Chapter Twenty-Four

When the fighting broke out Ethan and one other started boxing in Wynter and Anthony. Anthony recognized the second guy, Parker he thought the guy's name was. He was the ring leader who wanted Anthony evicted from the South Pole after Wynter left. It wasn't like Anthony had any intentions of staying anywhere where Wynter was not anyway. It didn't change the bad blood between them though.

Parker set his sights on Anthony. Anthony didn't know if that was to distract him from Ethan and Wynter or if Parker just had it in for him.

Ethan took a slow, methodical step toward Wynter wearing a look that she had only seen on his face one other time, the night she left the South Pole.

"Ethan why are you doing this?" she asked.

"Why should I show you mercy when you showed me none?"

"I never hurt you."

"Another one of your pretty lies except you're only lying to yourself now, princess. That's all you are, isn't it? A North Pole princess."

"Ethan, please," Wynter begged. The last thing she wanted was to fight Ethan.

"What were you even doing down there? You didn't belong."

"I needed… I don't know. I just needed something."

"I hope it was worth all the lives you ruined."

"I never meant to hurt anyone, especially you."

"Too late for that. By the time we get through here tonight, you'll be as friendless in this world as I am."

"That can't be true, Ethan. You must have friends."

"I have NO friends. No one trusts the fool who fell for your lies. You should be quite pleased with yourself. You lied from the very beginning, and I never even suspected. Tell me one thing, Wynter. Did Anthony know the truth?"

"He… he figured it out," she sighed.

"That first time we went to his house, that day he seduced you, did he know then?"

Wynter nodded in defeat, knowing that this wouldn't end well, wherever Ethan was going with it.

"I was scared for you! I was worried. I wanted to protect you. Oh, how you two must have laughed over that one!"

"It wasn't like that."

"Of course it was! Why did you pretend to let me teach you magic?"

"I wanted a friend so badly. I was alone."

"I don't believe you. The whole world loves jolly old St. Nickolas. I won't fall for your lies anymore."

"It's the truth! The whole world loves my father, but I was stuck here alone where everyone was too busy to spend time with me. I was ignored. I felt insignificant."

"You thought that coming down to the South Pole and playing us for fools would get you Daddy's attention."

"No! I would give anything to take back the hurt I caused you."

"Nothing but pretty lies."

"I had your number from the very beginning," Parker told Anthony. "You were in league with that Clause girl. I knew when you left us, you'd go running back to her."

"Yes, you've got us. It was an elaborate scheme to destroy the South Pole. Oh, wait. We left the South Pole just the way we found it… judgmental as ever," Anthony deadpanned.

"I think you've forgotten it was the Clauses you were hiding from in the first place."

"Why would I have been hiding from the Clauses when I truly believed they were the only ones who could help me? I was hiding from the monster inside myself."

"And now?" Parker challenged.

"Now I am a Clause."

"I knew you were no good from the moment I laid eyes on you."

"Then why don't you come over here and do something about it?"

Parker gave Anthony a lopsided grin, and the next thing Anthony knew there were three daggers flying in his direction. Anthony put his hand up to block the daggers and let them hit and fall to the ground as if they were no more than rubber toys.

Frustrated, Parker pulled out a gun and fired six times at Anthony's chest, but all that came out was water. Parker threw the useless water pistol to the ground and growled, "Stop that!"

"Did you really think that we would stand still while you murdered us?"

"You deserve to die."

"For many sins," Anthony admitted morosely. "I didn't realize that the South Pole had joined forced with the North Pole to seek justice against vampires."

Parker reached for a stake strapped to his leg. A wooden stake? Really? He lunged at Anthony clearly aiming for his heart.

"That's not who I am anymore," Anthony insisted grasping Parker's wrist and turning him about until he faced away from Anthony. Anthony held him there in a choke hold until Parker quit fighting. "You wanted me to leave the South Pole. Fine, I left. You have no business coming and attacking my family, and I will do whatever it takes to protect my family." Anthony tightened his grip around Parker's neck. "Do we understand each other?"

Parker tried to nod his head, but he must not have understood after all. As soon as Anthony let go, Parker turned, doubled over, and charged, ready to ram that big ugly head of his into Anthony's stomach. Anthony sidestepped and pushed Parker's head down to the ground as he ran past.

His head hit with a loud crack. Parker slumped to the ground, and blood pooled all around his head. Anthony flipped him over in order to check for a pulse. Faint, but it was there. Parker was alive, for now, but he was going to need medical attention.

"You don't look so alone now," Ethan accused Wynter.

"I'm not. I have Anthony, Noel, and even Roscoe. I worked things out with my parents, but mainly it helps that I have a life of my own now."

"So, you got your happily ever after at our expense."

"No, it wasn't like that."

"Just stop. Noah may believe all your lies, but I won't be so easily manipulated again."

"Can't we sit down and talk?" Wynter pleaded.

"The time for talk is over," he said as he took a menacing step closer.

"Wynter?" Anthony broke in.

Wynter didn't take her eyes off of Ethan. His head wasn't in a good place right now. He wasn't himself. Then to prove Wynter right, Ethan pulled a small gun from his coat pocket. He pointed it in Wynter's general vicinity, but before he could even aim it, the gun began to melt right there in his hand. The metal turned red as if inflamed. Ethan quickly dropped the gun and shook out his hand.

Wynter knew that she hadn't done that, but who had. She looked around to see Anthony glaring at Ethan. "I don't want to hurt a friend, Ethan, but if you become a threat to her, I will," Anthony warned.

"You're all one big happy family," Ethan sneered.

"That's right. We are. So is Noah, and Wynter wants nothing more than for you to be a part of that family as well."

Instead of answering Ethan dropped to the ground and pressed his hand into the snow.

"Ethan?" Wynter encouraged.

"We'll never be family. You're a Clause."

Tears ran down Wynter's cheeks when she finally realized that Ethan would never forgive her.

"You're an idiot," Anthony said barely above a whisper. "Not for coming here today thinking you stood a chance, but that was stupid too. No, you're an idiot for not seeing everything you had when it was right in front of you. She loved you, I mean really loved you. You could have had everything. A wonderful wife, a beautiful little girl, amazing in-laws, it could have all been yours. You were her first crush. You had everything I ever wanted, and you didn't even notice. I guess in that sense, I should be thanking you. I got to marry the love of my life, because you never really saw her and everything she was capable of."

"I don't want the love of a Clause."

"Then leave," Wynter said putting on a brave face. "You have no business here. Go home and never return."

"Not until I get what I came here for."

"And, what is that?"

"Revenge."

"Then mission accomplished. Leave," Anthony ordered. With a wave of Anthony's hand Ethan disappeared.

"Where is he?" Wynter sobbed.

"South Pole... I think," Anthony answered.

"NO!" Santa bellowed as he ran past Anthony and Wynter.

When they looked to see what had Santa in such an uproar they saw Vivienne and Mary chasing after a man who must have gotten past everyone and was headed in the direction of Mrs. Clause and Noel. Anthony and Wynter both joined in the chase.

"Wynter, I'll help Santa. Get to Noel and your mom," Anthony told her.

In a flash Wynter was inside her house and frantically looking for her mom and daughter. "Mom!... Noel!"

"In here," Mom called from Noel's room. "Is it all over?"

"No, he's headed this way. Get behind me."

Mrs. Clause swooped Noel up and clutched her to her chest then stood behind Wynter ready to attack anyone who came through the door.

❄ ❄ ❄

Mary was fast, but Vivienne was faster. Mary had traveled the world, but Vivienne had spent her entire life trudging through deep snow and ice. She over took Mary and caught up to the first man in no time.

Vivienne tackled the man from behind shoving him face first into the snow. When he came up for air, Vivienne flipped him over, pulled back, and punched him across the face.

Mary pulled him back to his feet. "Now where did you think you were going?"

Vivienne wrapped her arms around the man's and held him up on his feet facing Mary. Mary punched him in the gut and said, "That was for thinking you were going to come here and hurt my family." Another punch. "And, that was thinking that you would sneak away to do more harm." A third punch. "And, that one was so that you don't forget the first two."

❄ ❄ ❄

Kyson didn't stand a chance catching up with the others by the time they realized two of the attackers had gotten away. He ran anyway. The first guy was long out of site, but Vivienne had caught up with the other and tackled him. She had the guy eating snow. Vivienne wasn't all barbed wire and thorns, but she was far from a push over either.

That guy never knew what hit him, but he should have. Kyson recognized the guy as one of the referees from when he had played peewee hockey. Vivienne's older brothers refereed too, and Vivienne was always hanging around the rink. She was the toughest chick in or around the rink. That was when Kyson first started falling for her, and he'd only fallen harder every day since.

If the guy had taken more notice of his surroundings back in those days, he would already have known all about Vivienne. Maybe then he wouldn't have been so stupid as to challenge her, and trying to sneak past her was definitely a challenge to Vivienne.

Kyson was actually impressed with the way Vivienne shared when she pulled the guy to his feet and let Mary have a crack at him. Those two were going to be inseparable. Kyson could see it already. Which was fine, Kyson didn't begrudge her, her friends as long as those friends didn't take her away from the South Pole… They could visit one another, but if she ever moved away from the South Pole, Kyson would have no choice but to follow. Did that make him a creepy stalker type?

"There's another one," Mary alerted as her brother and Anthony drew nearer.

Anthony and Santa never broke stride. They kept running full out both on a mission. Anthony knew that

Wynter was there with Noel and that she would protect Noel with her dying breath, but who would protect Wynter? His best bet was to best the guy before he ever made it that far, but if he did make it as far as the house, Anthony knew he wouldn't hold back.

Santa ran as fast as he could for a jolly old fat man. He had known anger before in his life. Siblings could do that to you and especially head strong daughters, but he had never known anger as consuming as he was feeling now. He had never been tempted to kill, but he could do it now. That man was after his wife, his little girl, and his grandbaby, and the thought of murder was crossing his mind now. Santa would kill so that they could live.

Aldon ran as fast as he could. The Clauses were hiding something, something that they wanted protected more than themselves. The toy factory maybe? It didn't matter what it was. Aldon had made his escape, and he was going to find whatever they were hiding. Then he was going to destroy it.

Running through snow was tough, but Aldon was an expert. Recreational running was his sport of choice, and if the ice and snow of the South Pole couldn't slow

him down, the ice and snow of the North Pole certainly wouldn't.

At last a building that looked like a house became visible on the horizon. With his goal in sight, Aldon kicked up the speed. All his focus was on his goal, and he didn't see the bear until it was too late.

A huge polar bear jumped at him, knocking him to the ground and pinning him there. If this place was guarded by a freaking polar bear it must be what the Clauses were hiding. That was Aldon's last thought before the bear's claws began swiping. Again and again, the claws raked through his skin painfully. His face, his arms, his legs, Aldon was sure that the bear had hit several vital organs in his chest as well. So, this was how he was going to die.

He knew coming to the North Pole, that death was an option, but he had vowed to himself that he would not die without a fight. Somehow he pulled the gun from the holster around his waist. He held the gun in front of him the best he could and fired until the gun was empty.

What felt like a lifetime later the bear fell away. Aldon pushed to his feet. He couldn't see anything but red. He couldn't feel anything but pain. Still, a vow was a vow, and he was going to keep going until he took his last breath. Slowly he pulled himself through the doorway to the building. The smell of cookies hit him when he walked through the door. Funny that he could still smell. This must have been where the elves lived. Now to find those little buggers.

❄ ❄ ❄

"Come out, come out, wherever you are," a man sing-songed as he kicked the door in and walked through the back door. He wasn't even trying to be quiet. "I know you're in here, and I'm going to find you."

Then come on, Wynter thought to herself.

"Oh little elves?" the guy called.

He had to be kidding! This guy actually thought he was in the toy factory looking for elves? Did this look like any sort of factory to him? The truth was he was nowhere near the toy factory, and it was a good thing too. The elves were still working away in the factory as if nothing were askew. The elves wouldn't be of much use in a fight, so no one thought to disrupt the elves.

As the man strolled closer to Noel's room where Wynter stood with her mom and daughter behind her, Wynter couldn't resist the urge to mess with the guy's

mind a little. Ethan should really gather a better army next time.

Wynter put her hand in front of her face palm facing the ceiling. When the man stepped in front of her she blew across her hand as if blowing fairy dust. It wasn't until after that she saw the state of the man. He was covered in blood and long gaping wounds.

"There you are," the man gasped in surprise, and for a minute Wynter thought that her magic hadn't worked. "You do exist. I never believed until now that the elves were real."

The man turned a circle looking at all the elves, because right now he was taking a virtual reality tour of the toy factory.

"Wynter!" Anthony called as he walked through the splintered doorway. "What is he doing?"

"He thought he was in the toy factory, so I thought I'd give him a little tour, virtual reality."

"You're going to be the death of me, Wynter Clause," Anthony smiled and pulled Wynter against his chest.

"I saw my whole life flash before me when Mary said there was another one, and I must say I've been a very lucky man. I love you, Mrs. Clause," Santa said.

"I love you too, Santa dear."

"Elves!" Noel squealed and clapped for the man. Then as many as a dozen elf dolls the elves had fashioned especially for Noel all floated into the air and began to dance about.

Wynter breathed a sigh of relief, glad for the miracle that Noel didn't understand what was going on. Then she took Noel from Mrs. Clause, and Anthony secured the last attacker so that they could meet up with the others.

The man was going to need medical attention as well as Roscoe. Roscoe was bleeding and unresponsive. It was going to crush Wynter and Noel if anything happened to that big bear.

"What happened to him?" Vivienne asked as she ran in the room.

"I believe Roscoe got him… the polar bear," Anthony answered.

"I'm an ER nurse, but I'm going to need supplies." No sooner than Vivienne asked a first aid kit appeared by her side. "Wow, I wish it always worked that quickly."

"Anything you need, just ask. One of us can get it for you," Wynter informed.

"Wynter…" Anthony started, but he just didn't know how to tell her about Roscoe.

"Where's Roscoe?" she asked.

"Outside," Santa answered faintly.

"No," Wynter reacted and ran outside still holding Noel. Anthony was hot on her heels unsure what to do but be there.

When they got outside, Noah was bent down at Roscoe's side. Tears slid unbidden down Wynter's face.

"Roscoe, wake up!" Noel giggled.

"Oh, baby," Wynter cried. She looked around and spotted her parents. She handed Noel off to her dad and said, "Please, get her out of here." Then she dropped down in the blood tainted snow next to Noah. Anthony knelt down next to Wynter and wrapped himself around her.

"He's alive," Noah said.

He was alive. Noah had not said Roscoe would be okay, only that he was alive… for now. Wynter laid her head against his warm fur and sobbed for her friend. If he died, he died protecting Noel. Befriending a beast, a natural predator, was one of the best decisions Wynter had ever made.

"I need to get the bullets out," Noah told her.

"You can do that?"

"I'm a ranger. I know animals and how to care for them."

"Get her out of here, bloodsucker. I'll stay and help the kid," Aunt Mary said from above them.

Anthony pulled Wynter to her feet, and led her away. Wynter felt like she was in a fog and went wherever he led.

Chapter Twenty-Five

Later in Santa's living room the thirteen attackers
sat restrained and gagged but cozy enough in front of a
roaring fire. The only one missing was Ethan. Noah had
borrowed Santa's satellite phone to get in touch with his
parents, and they assured him that Ethan was at home
safe and sound, a little scared but safe none the less.

Parker was fine. Vivienne had tended to his minor
head wound as she had called it. Aldon was a different
story. He had been touch and go there for a while, but
in the end he was going to recover just fine. He would
forever carry the battle scars with him, and none of the
Clauses felt inclined to help him in that regard. Roscoe,
it seemed, had done more damage to Aldon than Aldon
had done to him. Roscoe was at Anthony and Wynter's
right now sleeping off his adventure in the living room

in front of a roaring fire. Noah had removed the bullets, and Mary had used magic to speed the healing process. Roscoe was lucky, Noah had said, because Aldon had failed to hit anything vital.

The other sixteen sat in various places around the room. Noel snoozed in Lorelei's lap after bonding easily with the girl from the South Pole. Noah sat close beside them using Noel as his excuse, but no one was fooled.

Declan and Aunt Star were sharing a recliner, a little too cozy if you asked Wynter.

Mary and Vivienne had been swapping stories for the last few minutes and giggling like school girls anytime Kyson looked their way.

Wynter was curled up in Anthony's lap. He didn't seem to be letting her go any time soon, and that was fine by Wynter. It had been a long day, full of emotional turmoil.

"Okay, if no one else wants to get this started then I will," Santa announced. "I think it is high time we got things settled once and for all."

"I do too," Lorelei agreed. "Before there's anymore fighting."

"So, what do we do?" Noah asked.

"You're a ranger now. Haven't you ever had to negotiate peace?" Anthony asked him a bit sarcastically.

"You're not going to get everyone to give up their prejudice," Enoch pointed out.

"No, I guess not," Santa gave in.

"What can both sides agree to then?" Israel asked.

"How about a peace treaty?" Star suggested. "You know, they don't have to like us, but if they don't, stay away. We promise peace as long as they do the same."

"Sounds fair," Mrs. Clause acknowledged. "You'll sign it won't you, dear?"

"Yes, of course, as long as that's what we all agree on." Santa looked around to all his brothers and sisters as well as Anthony and Wynter. Everyone nodded their approval.

"Good, draw something up, Wynter," Mrs. Clause instructed.

Wynter thought about it a moment then with a wiggle of her fingers a paper floated down into her father's lap. It said:

On this the twenty-fifth day of March two thousand seventeen,

The North Pole and South Pole do here by agree to a general peace. Neither side shall attack the other without just cause lest the treaty by null and void.

________________________________   ____________

Signature   date

________________________________   ____________

Signature   date

Santa signed on the first line and dated then handed the document to Noah.

"Why me?" Noah asked.

"You're a ranger. Why not you?" Lorelei encouraged. "I think you should have one of the others sign it too though," she added with a significant look to the South Polers sitting in front of the fire.

"Parker seems to carry a lot of pull down there. Let him sign," Anthony suggested.

Noah signed and dated then handed the paper to Parker, who Joseph had unbound and loosened his gag.

Parker signed without argument.

"Good, now that's done, what do you say we load you all into the sleigh, and I'll give you all a ride back to the South Pole," Santa offered.

"Sounds good to me," Kyson sighed. "I could use a good night's sleep in my own bed."

The trip back home was much more pleasant and extremely faster in Santa's sleigh. "So, Vivienne," Kyson started, "what did you think of the experience?"

"I had fun believe it or not. I even made plans with Mary to go vampire hunting."

"You're leaving the South Pole?"

"Nah, just a vacation here and there."

"That's a vacation?" Enoch laughed.

"Mary did have some advice for me that was really sound," Vivienne continued.

"What's that?" Kyson asked curiously.

Vivienne leaned across the sleigh and pressed her lips to Kyson's. "Quit waiting on you to make the first move. Life is too short to waste."

"You know, I think I like Mary."

Joseph, Israel, and North hit the road soon after Santa all eager to get home to their families.

"I'm going to miss that guy," Star remarked.

"You took a liking to him," Mrs. Clause observed.

"I've never seen you that attached to a guy," Mary remarked.

"Yeah, maybe it's the guy. Maybe it's the novelty of the South Pole. Now that there's a peace between us, I might take him up on his offer to visit sometime."

"Not everyone down there will be so friendly," Wynter reminded her.

"I know, but it would still be nice to visit just once," Star sighed.

"Listen, I'm going to excuse myself from all the girl talk, but first Mary, I just wanted to thank you," Anthony said.

"I didn't do it for you, bloodsucker... You do take good care of my niece. Maybe you're not all bad, but this doesn't mean that I forgive you."

Anthony nodded and left the room.

"I wish you'd give him a break, Aunt Mary. He's trying," Wynter said.

"I can see that now."

"Well, it's about time," Star laughed.

Wynter's relationship with Aunt Mary would never be what it once was. Wynter didn't think that she could ever erase from her memory the things Aunt Mary had said to Anthony, and she was sure that Aunt Mary could never erase her memories of Anthony. They had found a peace, though. That was enough for now. It was a foundation to build on, and maybe one day instead of renewing an old relationship, they would strengthen a new one.

Chapter Twenty-Six

"Daddy funny!" Noel giggled as Anthony fumbled with the harness.

"I'm never going to get this," Anthony fretted.

"It took me a month just to learn the harnesses. You're doing fine," Santa encouraged.

Anthony looked to Wynter trying to read her face, but Wynter was currently making goofy faces at Blitzen. The little trader. Blitzen had stood diligently by Anthony's side until he reached for the harnesses. Then she turned tail.

Donner was staring at Anthony with a look that could only be described as told you so. Oh, if that reindeer could talk! Anthony was sure that he would give everyone grief and boss the others around. You couldn't much complain, though; Donner was an excellent leader for the team and kept them all on pace.

Dancer and Prancer weren't paying anyone any attention except for Noel here and there when she would join in their frolicking. The three of them made quite a team dancing about the ice. Dancer was pretty good. Prancer and Noel simply shook their backsides, which was cute on Noel.

Cupid was the kiss up. She was watching everything Anthony and Santa did with rapt attention. He acted as if this was all vital information that he might need one day. Then again, if Anthony goofed, it might be a good idea to have someone along who knew what they were doing.

Vixen, the flirt, kept nudging Anthony and Santa in the face or shoulder. That didn't make working a harness any easier.

"Now you've got it!" Santa exclaimed. Anthony didn't know what he had or how he had done it. "Now try putting it on one of them."

"Blitzen, come here, girl," Anthony called.

Blitzen snorted at Wynter one last time then trotted over. She stood perfectly still while Anthony clumsily fitted the harness to her back.

"I'll never know how you get her to stand so still for so long," Wynter marveled.

"Now you've done it. All that's left is to harness the others and strap them together," Santa said with a jolly laugh.

"All that's left?" Anthony repeated feeling defeated.

Just then Blitzen took off in a sprint with Anthony still holding fast to her back. In the wink of an eye, Blitzen took to the sky and brayed loudly in a victory call. Santa and Wynter rolled with laughter while Noel clapped and hollered, "Daddy go! Daddy go!"

"What is that Blitzen is dragging?" Mrs. Clause asked walking up on the scene.

"That's Anthony," Wynter cackled.

"Merciful heavens! Someone get him down from there."

"No need, dear. Anthony can handle Blitzen better than the two of us ever could. Watch this," Santa said gesturing to where Blitzen was softly touching back down on the ice.

"Good girl," Anthony cooed.

Mrs. Clause just shook her head and said, "I knew if I left it up to you, you three would never come in for lunch, so I brought lunch out to you. Anthony, quit playing around and come eat. Noel, come see what Gam brought you to eat."

It took Anthony another hour after lunch to finish harnessing the other reindeer and an additional forty-five minutes to strap them together.

"There, so much for the easy part," Santa huffed in satisfaction.

"The easy part?" Anthony reacted.

"Oh yes. Now you have to not only get the reindeer to listen to your command but to do it at the same time and work as a team. That is no easy feat on the best of nights. Now, into the sleigh you go."

Anthony gave Wynter a worried look, but he would get no sympathy from her. In return, she gave him a nod of encouragement and a shove toward the sleigh. He climbed inside, held the reigns in his hands, and took a deep calming breath.

"Now Donner, Dancer now, Prancer and Vixen. On Comet, on Cupid, Dasher and Blitzen!" Anthony called with a confident voice. At once the team lurched forward and took to the air.

"I wouldn't have believed it if I hadn't have seen it with my own eyes," Santa breathed. "Even my own father couldn't handle the reindeer that fine. The kid's a natural."

"He sure is," Wynter smiled with pride.

"I go, Daddy! I go!" Noel screamed after him.

Anthony did a couple of laps before coming back down only long enough for Wynter to hand Noel up.

Epilouge

Noah had asked Lorelei out on their very first date. He was surprised she'd said yes. Now he just had to make everything perfect.

They were staying at his house, since there were still so many people mad at them for everything that had happened, but this would die down. Eventually everything would go back to normal. Until then the best date was one spent at home.

Noah was grilling, because really that was the best thing he could cook. He had steaks, baked potatoes, and vegetable kabobs. It wasn't an overly romantic meal, but at least it was edible. That was really saying something for a meal he cooked on his own with no help from his mother.

He wasn't picking her up. She was coming here. As far as Noah was concerned that was already a check in the negative column. The guy should pick the girl up for the perfect first date. Lorelei was adamant, though, there was no sense in him picking her up just to turn around and go back home.

Here he was pacing the floor. Noah flung the door open as soon as the doorbell rang. The thought to act casual never even crossed his mind. If she was alarmed or disturbed by his too quick answer, it didn't show.

"Hey," she greeted.

"Hey, come in. I grilled some steaks. I hope that's okay."

"That sounds delicious."

Noah led her into the kitchen where he had the table decorated with candles and a tablecloth he had borrowed from his mom.

"How's Ethan?" Lorelei asked.

"He's still pouting, mad. I think he's embarrassed more than anything."

"Do you think he and Wynter will ever be friends again?"

"I don't know. It's hard to tell."

"How are your parents taking it?"

"They're just glad Ethan is all right. I think it is finally hitting them how badly it could have ended and how lucky we all are that the Clauses are such good people."

"Yeah, I liked them. Noel is the cutest thing I've ever seen."

"Yeah, I want one just like her one day. I mean, uh..."

Did he really just say that on a first date? He was going to scare her off.

Lorelei just laughed. "Noah, it's okay that you want to have kids someday. There's nothing wrong with that."

"I just didn't want to..."

"Rush me? It's okay. We have time." She gave him a big smile and sat down at the table.

Noah grinned; everything was going to turn out just fine after all. "You know, I think my parents are actually relieved."

"What do you mean?"

"Well, Mom never wanted to talk about Wynter before, and now Wynter is all she can talk about, at least when Ethan's not around. She wants to know how she's doing now. If she's happy? Is she healthy? How old Noel is and everything I can remember about her. It's almost…"

"Almost what?"

"It's almost like the prodigal son has come home. Even Dad is different. He doesn't join Ethan in the Clause bashing anymore. Any time Wynter's name comes up he reminds Ethan, 'She spared your life, son, when none of us were willing to do the same for her.' Then he changes the subject. I guess that he's ashamed that Wynter Clause had to set the example for everyone, himself included. He's happier too, happier than I've seen him since Wynter left. He never brings her up except to shut Ethan up, but I know he listens when Mom asks about her."

"Noah… do you think they never really hated her."

"I don't know. They supported Ethan. For a while there I thought we'd face Dad in the North Pole too."

"I know, but that was what was expected of them. What if they pretended to hate her out of some sense of duty? As South Polers it was their place to hate the Clauses? Could it be that it was all an act, and deep in their heart they still loved her? You said she was like a daughter to them once. Maybe, for them, this is like getting back the daughter they lost?"

"I never thought of it that way. It's possible I guess... How are things with Riana?"

Lorelei gave a long suffering sigh. "She's as Riana as ever. We had a meeting today to discuss how things are not working out. We're simply too different," Lorelei mocked. "I have a month to decide which of us will find a new place. A month's notice before I get kicked out? All in all it could have gone a lot worse. Too bad I'm more than likely going to be back in my parents' place."

"Things that bad at the shop?"

"Yes and no," Lorelei answered with a winning smile that made Noah's heart melt. "My customers are enraged... just not enough to walk. They said and I quote, 'It's just so hard to find anyone else that does my hair the way I like it.'"

"That's great!"

"It is."

"So, why are you moving back in with your parents?"

"Noah, your place is great, and you got a wonderful deal on it. But, deals like that don't happen often.

Apartments are scarce in this area, which makes them super expensive."

"You're welcome here."

"Thanks, but that would be uncomfortable with us dating. I wish I could wave my hand and build a house like the Clauses."

"Maybe you should write Santa and ask for a house for Christmas."

"Very funny."

"If you don't like that, we could always… get married?"

❄ ❄ ❄

It turned out that Eddie liked keeping the books for Lorelei's shop, and he took a personal interest in the people. In the end, he decided to invest, and they became partners.

Blossom later apologized for "chickening out." She was sorry that it ever had to come down to a fight but grateful that no one had been killed. She wanted desperately to pledge her loyalty from here on out but admitted that she couldn't handle fighting.

Stewart, Milo, Owen, Everett, and Carlisle were all astounded that a peace treaty was signed by either

party. They also let it be known that they never believed it would last. Vivienne told them in no uncertain terms that they could "shove it."

Enoch stayed in touch with Joseph Clause. He's even planning a trip to America in the summer. He wasn't the only one to keep in touch either. Declan and Star were now devoted pen pals.

And, of course, Kyson and Vivienne's story was only just beginning.

❄ ❄ ❄

Nine months later, "I won't be here to help you get Noel to bed," Anthony fretted.

"Would you stop worrying? Everything is going to be fine."

"It's just that this is my first time out on my own, you know?"

"It's also going to be the first Christmas Eve I've ever spent with my dad, ever. You'll do great. You'll be back in the morning, and I've got a big Christmas surprise waiting on you."

"I hope you're right," Anthony said before kissing his wife and daughter good bye.

He climbed onto the sleigh. It was crowded with toys. When he returned, it would be a big, empty, lonely sleigh. He called all the reindeer by name and waved good bye to everyone he left behind in the North Pole.

The reindeer took off without a hitch. Working with the reindeer would be the easiest part of the night to come. He was excited but nervous. He was doing it. He was really doing it. He was Santa. That was difficult to wrap his mind around. Anthony Phillips, vampire turned Santa? It was more than a dream come true, because he had never once in all his life ever thought to dream so big.

All around the world boys and girls were asleep in their beds waiting for him to deliver. He couldn't let them down. There was a route mapped out. Everything was bagged, tagged, and organized. It was all dummy proof. He just had to do it.

After the first couple houses, he started to calm. After the first couple thousand, he was in a groove. The whole night slipped by in the flash of an eye, and as the sun rose on the new fallen snow, Anthony landed back in the North Pole where Santa and Wynter waited to help him with the reindeer. Anthony bounded down from the sleigh with a joyful smile that he could do nothing to wipe away, and he didn't want to.

"How did it go?" Santa asked.

"It was wonderful!" Anthony exclaimed.

"I knew you'd do great," Wynter said with confidence.

"Is Noel still asleep?" Anthony inquired.

"She woke up just a few minutes ago. Mom is entertaining… I brought you a little something." Wynter handed Anthony a small rectangular box as she pulled him back behind the stables.

"What is this?"

"Open it and see."

Anthony tore off the paper and pulled open the lid. Inside nestled among the tissue paper was a pregnancy test showing a little pink plus sign.

"Is this what I think? Are we having another baby?"

"Merry Christmas," Wynter said and kissed him soundly.

Also Available From Elizabeth Lee Sorrell

Wrong Turn Fairy Tales

Gwynn worked hard to live up to her family's expectations putting away all childish things and even a few childhood friends. Now she is about to marry Addison, a very sensible, very rich businessman, but before she can say yes to his proposal, she finds herself falling through one fairy tale after another. Will she find her happily ever after with her very own prince charming, or has her fairy tale taken a wrong turn?

Exclusively found from Barnes & Nobles for Nook Book.

More Than Instinct

Kat had a past best left forgotten. Jackson had a past he couldn't get over, but when circumstances throw them together in a dangerous game, they had to find a way to work together. What they would find was that, "This whole mess had bonded them in a way that could never be undone."

Available from your favorite bookstore.

Black & White

Shantelle White has been with a top secret branch of the CIA from its very beginning. Jayson Black is one of the branches top operatives. When funds get tight Shantelle and Jayson are forced together to find a solution. Will they find out where the money has gone and who is behind it before all their agents are gone?

Available from your favorite bookstore.

About the Author

Elizabeth Lee Sorrell is an Alabama native. A gifted teacher, she has worked with babies and preschoolers, from her teens all the way to today. She is a teacher in the Federal Head Start program. She has her Associate's Degree in Early Childhood Development, her Bachelor's in Early Childhood Education and Elementary Education, and her Master's in Early Childhood Education.

When not teaching, or leading as the Nursery Coordinator of her church, she is with her family and dear friends, probably reading or writing a book. She loves to spend time with her nieces. Elizabeth is a Christian. She cheers for the Auburn Tigers, and the Atlanta Braves. As a big baseball fan, she has, more than once, written stories in the world of MLB, and watches as many games as she is able.

She enjoys pairing up with Sandra JS Coleman for her covers and illustrations. Sandra, Elizabeth's sister, is a graphic designer and an illustrator.

Learn more at www.ElizabethLeeSorrell.com

Colophon

Cover Design, Cover Photography, and interior
layout designed by Sandra JS Coleman using
Adobe CC software.

The typefaces used on the cover and interior are
Azo Sans Uber, Marydale and Mrs Eaves OT.

Azo Sans Uber was designed by Rui Abreu. He is a
Portuguese type and graphic designer, working on
commercial fonts since 2006. Marydale was designed
by Bryan Willson in 1993. It was his first font designed
based on a friend's handwriting. Mrs Eaves was designed
by Zuzana Licko in 1996. Licko emigrated to the US in
1968 and graduated from Berkeley in 1984.

The book was printed in the United States of America,
on 50lb white paper, perfect bound, with a gloss cover.

9 780999 580011